# Portraits of the Missing
## Imaginary Biographies

# *Portraits*
# *of the Missing*
## Imaginary Biographies

# Julian Symons

ANDRE DEUTSCH

First published in 1991 by
André Deutsch Limited
105-106 Great Russell Street London WC1B 3LJ

ISBN 0 233 98718 5

Phototypeset by Falcon Graphic Art Ltd
Wallington, Surrey
Printed by Billing & Sons, Worcester

*In memory of Geoffrey and Jane Grigson*

# Contents

# Preface

THE PEOPLE WHOSE lives are sketched here resemble a little the composite figures made up in those play books for children called Heads, Bodies and Legs, where the head of a philosopher, the body of a monkey and the legs of a giraffe may be put together to make a figure. Nothing similarly grotesque is attempted in this collection but the characteristics of two or three people have gone to the making of each biography along with fragments of their lives, and the element of imagination is not lacking. Ella is the composite of a girl I knew at school, a publisher's editor and the relict of a writer, Mr Jacob a blend of two men who cut my hair. Rupert Loxley is probably the most nearly recognisable of the characters, but there are aspects of the imaginary life not replicated in the real one. The identification of any single individual would be misleading or false.

The pieces have origins both personal and social. Every writer has met people he itched to characterise on paper, whether out of love, admiration, dislike, or simply as an example of the vagaries in human personality. Somerset Maugham said it was universal among writers of fiction to work from the living model, although this should surely be modified to working *away* from a living model, if only from fear of libel. Yet there are people who obstinately refuse to be characterised, either from some failure of the writer's perceptiveness, or because their lives and qualities seem unsuitable for shaping into his particular fictions. In that sense, these might be called characters never fitted into any of my crime stories.

They are informed also, however, by the intention of making social points always likely to be present in the writing of a man of the Thirties. The sketches are concerned with ways of life and attitudes to society alien, perhaps incomprehensible, to anybody under the age of forty. The ambitions and defeats of these partly fictional figures, and the failure of their early beliefs, have many parallels in historical fact, and for that reason alone seemed worth putting down.

As to the approach, the blending of reality and fiction, I am conscious of two particular debts. The lesser one is to Arthur Symons's *Spiritual Adventures*, one among his several unjustly neglected books. The account of Peter Waydelin, 'the painter of those mysterious, brutal pictures, who died last year at the age of twenty-four', and in his death agony tried to draw the wife whose 'pose, its grotesque horror, were finer than the finest of his inventions', particularly impressed me. But Arthur Symons's adventures were spiritual, those of my people mundane. A more considerable debt is to Max Beerbohm's *Seven Men*, that masterly blend of fact and fiction called by his publisher, far too crudely, short stories. I have used Beerbohm's devices of adding verisimilitude by the introduction of known names among the imagined ones, and by putting the subjects into the context of the writer's own life. It is in the Café Royal and through William Rothenstein that Beerbohm meets the archetypal Nineties poet Enoch Soames, buys his volume of poetry *Negations*, and is later sceptical of Rothenstein's claim that Soames does not exist. James Pether is met by the author at the casino in Dieppe, and he remembers A. V. Laider while recuperating from influenza in a small hotel by the sea.

Beerbohm has been my guide, although not my model. The original *Seven Men* contained only six sketches. The seventh man, unnoticed but omnipresent, and with his own personality implicitly conveyed, was the author. A similarly elusive figure offers fragments of real or imaginary autobiography here.

Several of these pieces have appeared in the *London Magazine*, and I am grateful to Alan Ross both for his encouragement of this project and for permission to reprint.

# E. J. Bastable and the Poet of the Era

FEW PEOPLE NOWADAYS will remember the name of E. J. Bastable, yet in my youth it was familiar to anybody who read the book pages of the serious Sunday papers, or looked at the weeklies. In the *Spectator* and *Time and Tide* Bastable wrote, perhaps once a month, a column for which the now almost obsolete word *causerie* is apt. These chatty general pieces of some fifteen hundred words dealt occasionally with subjects that might be called offshoots of literature (how many times Ruskin visited Venice was one, Theobald's emendations of Shakespeare another), but more often with such matters as the pleasures of spending an unforeseen three or four hours in Crewe, or the eccentric bookseller Bastable had come across in Woking. He would speculate whimsically on the reasons why doctors' writing was so often illegible, describe the pleasures of walking from his home in Hampstead to Fleet Street . . . Yes, *causerie* is the only word.

In the Sunday papers he reviewed perhaps twice a month, in the early part of his career – that is, immediately after World War I and in the early Twenties – mostly writing about such minor Victorian poets as Lord de Tabley, Alice Meynell and John Davidson, with excursions into discussion of Henley, Stevenson, Francis Thompson, when studies of them were published. By the early Thirties, when I first encountered his name, Bastable had shifted ground from poetry to the novel. He was the man naturally called on to write about Meredith, Wilkie Collins, Thackeray, Charles Reade – or Galsworthy, Bennett, Wells, Walpole. Ralph Straus ruled the fictional roost

I

in the *Sunday Times*, Gerald Gould in the *Observer*, in relation to 'modern literature' – which meant mostly the latest best-seller – but in those days of wide margins and large type there was plenty of room for Bastable. His reviews were long and often seemed longer, but I rarely read them through to the end.

One day in the summer of 1936 I was telephoned by my brother AJ, who asked if I could come round to the First Edition Club for a glass of sherry after leaving my engineering office. Such invitations, I knew from the past, usually meant that there was something AJ needed, either information about one of the modern literary figures outside his ken as a dedicated Victorian, or a book that had to be delivered to or collected from some remote bit of London which he was confident I knew. Usually, but not invariably. There were other times when AJ simply wanted to do me a good turn by effecting an introduction to somebody who might help to get me away from the drudgery of my job with Victoria Lighting and Dynamos, into the pleasanter fields of editing or book reviewing.

And so it proved this time. In the elegant former vestry of St George's Bloomsbury, where the First Edition Club of which he was the sole director was housed, AJ dispensed sherry from a decanter with customary gravity, and said 'This is Ernest Bastable'. A hand touched mine, and after a moment's confusion – I had to translate the initials I knew into 'Ernest' – I realised that this was truly Bastable the reviewer.

He was a very tall man, as tall as AJ who stood six foot three, and astonishingly thin. No doubt his clothes fitted, but they seemed to hang on him. The hand that had touched mine was so nearly skeletal that one had the impression anything involving a grip would have been beyond the power of those brittle fingers. His hair was very thin, and combed carefully across a white scalp to which the few strands appeared adhesively fixed, with the features beneath etiolated, bloodless as if he had been kept for several years indoors. (In view of his multifold reviewing activities that might indeed have been the case, but there were the walks from Hampstead to Fleet Street, of which he looked quite incapable.) The ears were neat, small, close to the head, but the rest of the face although thin was curiously large, the forehead not broad but unquestionably steep, nose narrow yet in profile distinctly big, lips thin and pale, and the chin narrow – with so thin a face how could it have been otherwise? – yet continuing for some distance, and ending in a rather menacing point.

The eyes were perhaps the best feature. Large, almost lustrous, nut brown in colour, their eagerness seemed to belong to some different face altogether, they were eyes that demanded ruddy cheeks and good springy curly hair. The total impression was not feeble, as I may be conveying, but one of delicacy. Bastable was in his early fifties, but seemed to me much older. In a thin, reedy voice that went with the face and not the eyes, he said that he was delighted to meet me, and had heard a lot about me. I was surprised, slightly alarmed. What could AJ have been saying?

'I understand you are a formidable chess player.'

The words enlightened me. AJ liked all of his friends to have a particular talent, so that they could be introduced as an expert on (as it might be) heraldry, arms and armour, the history of dress, Napoleon's campaigns in Italy. This feeling was extended to his family, and I saw that I was cast in the role of first class chess player. Quite wrongly cast, for I was never even a good club player. AJ had been deceived by the fairly wide acquaintance I had then with chess gambits. He had come back from a day spent with Lord Alfred Douglas at Douglas's flat in Hove. In the course of the day they had played chess, and Douglas won by using the Muzio gambit, which he had assured AJ was unbeatable. The Muzio, which involves a dramatic early sacrifice by white, is a showy unsound gambit, long ago rejected as hopeless by any regular player. I assured AJ of this, demonstrated it by beating him when he used it, and had evidently been given verbal promotion which I now disclaimed.

'Julian underestimates himself', AJ said, adding that I

3

was also a modern poet of the usual unintelligible kind. Bastable paid no attention to this, but asked questions about which gambits I used, what I thought of the flexibility of the Ruy Lopez, whether I approved the restrictions of the Sicilian Defence, and so on. The fluency of my answers left Bastable nodding agreement and greatly impressed AJ who, pushing my cause a little perhaps, suggested that the two of us should have a game at some time. In his reedy voice, a little hesitantly, Bastable asked if I would consider travelling as far as – he paused, then brought it out – 'Hampstead?'. I said I would, he murmured something about what a pleasure that would be, and drifted away.

'Bastable knows everybody', AJ said reprovingly, when I had said that he seemed as dreary a man as he was a critic. 'He could introduce you to literary editors, he knows them all. And he is a talented fellow. He is writing a book on Henley.'

'The regatta?'

'The poet of empire.'

I expected to hear no more of Bastable, so it was a surprise to receive a week later a note, written in a bold sprawling hand, inviting me to supper. The note was signed 'Elena Bastable', and a postscript in the same bold hand said 'Quite informal, of course'.

At the time I was unused to such invitations, had never attended any dinner or supper party, was used only to the mildly bohemian kind of party at which everybody brought a bottle, there were fierce drink-induced arguments, and one or two people were sick, in the lavatory basin if the host was lucky. I realised the Bastables' hospitality would not be of that kind, but still carried a bottle of *vin ordinaire* wrapped in brown paper.

The Bastables lived in a small house just off Downshire Hill, and the door was opened by a maid in cap and apron.

4

Behind her, in a darkish hall, appeared Bastable, thin as a shadow. The depth of my error was apparent even to somebody as little couth as I was then. No doubt I should have put down the bottle and said nothing, but instead I thrust it at Bastable, who unwrapped it, looked at the label, and seemed at a loss for words. Finally he murmured, 'My dear fellow', handed the bottle to the maid, and led the way to a sitting room with french windows opening on to a small garden. He offered me a glass of sherry with the comment that I would of course recognise it as Tio Pepe. This was a reference to the fact that AJ, who was also secretary of the Wine and Food Society, had recently written an article pronouncing that sherry was the only tolerable drink before a meal, and that among sherries Tio Pepe was the most reliable.

He asked whether I was interested in gardens. I answered truthfully that I knew nothing about them. A silence ensued, which I knew to be awkward yet felt myself unable to break. Bastable sat looking out at the garden which I had deprived him of showing to me, his thin white fingers picking gently at the arm of his chair. I said I understood he was writing about W. E. Henley, and he brightened. What did I know about Henley?

The ploy had been rash, for the answer was that I had little knowledge and less interest, remembering only the poem about being 'Captain of my soul', and another which called death 'the ruffian on the stair'. However, this proved not to matter. Bastable stopped picking, and spoke with enthusiasm in his reedy voice of Henley's talent as an editor and his still unrecognised genius as a poet.

'He was the poet of an era, the laureate of the dying glories of empire.' I asked if the Nineties writers were not just as typical in a wholly different way, but he brushed this aside.

'They belonged to the past, the *fin-de-siècle*. Henley represented the future. It was a tragic irony that the healthy mind should have been housed in a diseased and broken body.' If it was said that people in general do not talk in this literary way I should agree, but it was the way that Bastable talked. He continued: 'There is always a poet supremely typical of the hopes and finest aspirations of an era. In the mid-Victorian age it was Tennyson, then Browning, and at the end it was Henley. They were the three poets of an era.'

I was saved from the need to comment by the arrival of Elena Bastable, who entered the room laughing, holding out both hands in greeting, apologising for her absence in the kitchen because of a minor crisis. She said all three things at once as it seemed, and managed to say in addition how pleased she was to meet me, Ernest who admired AJ so very much had come back and told her there was another amazingly talented person in the family, somebody who knew all the gambits, whatever gambits were. And so – well, so here I was.

Elena Bastable was very much like what her handwriting might have led me to expect, plump, energetic, talkative. She was also, as I might have foreseen from her name, central European, with a spontaneous jollity that is peculiarly unEnglish. Within a couple of minutes she was calling me Julian, saying I reminded her of a Roman Emperor of the same name – or was it a Pope? – hoping that Ernest had not been boring me by going on and on about his roses, and confessing that there really was a *crisis* in the kitchen, she must go away again or we would have nothing whatever to eat. We would have time for a game of chess before supper, she knew Ernest was longing for it – and then, as it seemed in mid-sentence, she had gone. Bastable gave a sweet, almost wistful smile, said Elena was truly amazing, and suggested that we should repair to his den.

This was a small room next door. The walls were lined with books which I should have liked to look at, but beside the desk Staunton pattern chessmen were laid out on a small table. The desk was enviably neat, a writing pad in the middle, pens in a rack just beyond, and a calendar with a small oblong card attached to it on the right. On the card, in large type, were the words 'Review needed', and beside them a well-drawn finger pointed to a date. I should have liked to ask whether this warning notice slid up, down and along, whether Bastable sometimes forgot to shift it and so was late in delivering a review, but our business was with the chess board. A chair had been placed for me, and Bastable shifted his desk chair round beside the board. His pallor was if possible accentuated, his thin lips even thinner, the menacing point at the end of his chin appeared to twitch.

Foolishly, I had given no thought to the prospect of playing chess against Bastable. From my point of view he was somebody who might be able to give me useful introductions or get me some reviewing. From his, as I now uncomfortably realised, I was only an opponent on the other side of a chess board. Within a few moves it was clear to me, and must have been plainer still to him, that my ability to talk with him on even terms about gambits had been a piece of unwitting deception. I have no idea how good a player he was, but a game between us was no contest. My defeat was quick and comprehensive. Bastable said I had not done myself justice, we must have another game, and perhaps I would not be offended if next time he gave me a rook. The pieces were set out when Elena rang a bell for supper.

I cannot remember what we ate, except that it was some central European dish, nor what was said beyond registering that Elena was wholly unintellectual, and seemed to regard her husband's reviewing activities as something that had to be done, as she had to do the cooking, but that he made an unnecessary fuss about it. The maid in cap and apron never reappeared, and I indulged a fantasy that she had been hired simply as a door-opener, to give a touch of the formality apparent in Bastable's grave pouring of the wine (my *vin ordinaire*, of course, had vanished like the maid), solemn approach of his large nose to it, slight raising of the eyebrows when I took a preliminary gulp. Elena noticed this.

'He is an old *fusspot*', she said. 'Pay no attention to him. I tell him drinking should be hearty, not in little sips. Like this.' And she drained her glass. 'You see he is laughing, I

7

can make the old fusspot laugh, that is why we love each other.' And although Bastable did not laugh he smiled and nodded, and said Elena was good for an old fogey. When I mentioned the book on Henley she flung up her hands.

'For years he has been doing Henley, I am sick of Henley. A book should not take years to write, don't you agree, Julian? You work on it, then you get it out of your system, it is over, you start another. Like a baby, only we have no babies.' Bastable frowned slightly, and put his nose in the glass. 'Ernest did not want them. He says you should not talk about such things, but for me there is nothing you cannot talk about. Young people today, they talk about everything, isn't that so?'

'If they do, it is because they are immature', Bastable said, but the rebuke implicit in the words was not endorsed by his accompanying look, which was full of sweetness.

Dinner over, Elena said indulgently that no doubt we wanted to go back to our game. She spoke like a mother to children. 'This time you beat him, you see. He thinks he is such a good player, you take him down a peg.'

We played two more games, and in the second Bastable gave me a queen, but I still lost. He was immensely polite, saying again that I had clearly not done myself justice, but I sensed his disappointment. My literary credentials, also, were far from being established, and with such establishment in mind I returned to Henley. If it was true that Henley was the poet of the late Victorian era, I said, wouldn't he agree that Auden was the poet of our modern era? Bastable considered this carefully.

'Perhaps I am not sufficiently – apprised – of recent poetic developments to say, but I have read some of W. H. Auden's poems. I know that many of you young people, even some critics, consider he is – the cat's pyjamas – but I could not agree. Oh no, I certainly could not agree. You will no doubt take my disagreement as the view of an old fogey, who requires that poetry should be beautiful in both thought and expression. I do not find such beauty in your friend Mr

8

Auden. I am not opposed to experiment, but for me poetry must – aspire. I understand that such a view is old-fashioned.'

I agreed with that last phrase, although I did not say so. After such remarks, and my ignominious failure at chess, I lacked heart to mention the possibility of some reviewing introduction. It had been a disastrous evening. AJ, when he asked for and received a report of it, showed his displeasure. What use was there in his arranging for me to meet a man who knew everybody, if I failed to live up to the reputation he had invented for me at chess?

A little later I sent out a circular inviting subscriptions to the little verse magazine I was preparing, *Twentieth Century Verse*. I sent out something like a thousand circulars, and remember clearly that I received nine subscriptions. One was from Bastable.

He wrote a little note to me after receiving each issue, saying that he admired a poem by Dylan Thomas, 'although to tell the truth I am not sure that I understood anything beyond each individual line', and approving pieces by John Pudney and Richard Church, 'even though I should hardly have thought these were "modern" poets as you use the word.' Reading these notes today I find them touching in their tentativeness, generous in their efforts to praise what must have been mostly uncongenial. At the time, though, I ridiculed them, reading out chosen passages to friends as examples of dreary middlebrow feebleness. Bastable also devoted most of one *causerie* to discussion of modern poetry 'as we find it in the new little magazines', deprecating the roughness and triviality of pieces that were 'clearly verse, not poetry', and calling for a poet who would 'transcend the ordinary, commonplace and practical, and take us into that realm of the spirit where poetry truly dwells.'

Then one day he sent me what he called 'a slender sheaf' of poems by somebody called Thomas Tucker, with an accompanying letter saying that for him these were perhaps the real thing. 'You will remember that we talked of the poet of the era. I truly believe he may be found in this young man.' It

9

seemed improbable that I should like a poet recommended by Bastable, and I put the slender sheaf among a pile of unread poems a couple of inches thick.

At that time I lived in a curious cellar in Pimlico's St George's Square, consisting of a single large and lofty room with no window but only a skylight, plus bedroom and kitchen. The cellar was in effect an extension built out from the house, and had its own separate entrance, with a spy hole (common now, but unusual then) through which visitors could be examined. I was expecting a visit from Ruthven Todd, who lived just across the Square, and when the bell rang opened the door without looking through the spy hole.

A tall man confronted me, his features in shadow. His arms flapped like a bird's wings, he spoke in a loud harsh voice.

'Great fallen angel, creature of the skies,
Straddling the earth with broad Promethean thighs,
What human art measures your monstrous size?'

I stood and peered at him. With a cawing laugh he said, 'I sing for my supper. And yet a song may last for ever, whether sung for supper or just for joy. You do not know me, but you know my poems.' I said something indicating incomprehension. 'Thomas Tucker. You have my poems.'

At that the wheels in my mind moved, as they should have done before, and I asked him in. He shrugged off the coat round his shoulders, dropped it on a chair. In the light he was revealed as scarecrow rather than predatory bird, tall and thin, arms poking out of a short-sleeved jacket, gaudy socks visible below short and slightly ragged trousers. His face was thin, hair dark, a small tic moved below his right eye. He took out a packet of cigarettes, tapped one on his thumbnail, and said 'Well?'

When I said I had not yet read his poems he gave another cawing laugh, unsurprised but contemptuous, and began to tell me what was wrong with my magazine.

'What all of you are afraid of is seriousness. You fear the metaphor, detest the metaphysical, caution is your watchword. You have no conception of the universe or of society. Have you read Vico?' I shook my head. 'Croce? Kierkegaard? I thought not. Truly is it said that where there is no vision the people perish, and by vision I don't mean – no, I do not mean – Hegelian idealism ending in a mess of petty compromises. I mean a system of knowledge finding its ultimate expression in a poetry that looks for the sublime . . .'

That is a fair example of his talk, which seemed to me unintelligible for the most part, occasionally perceptive, at other times almost insane. I was pleased when Ruthven arrived, but even the usually garrulous Ruthven was struck almost to silence by this brew of philosophy, religion, sociology and poetry. We went round the corner to the local Henekey's. There Tucker drank beer and ate a cheese roll without appearing to notice them, although he bought a round of drinks when it was his turn. He tended to brush aside personal matters, but in the course of the evening we learned that he lived near King's Cross, was unmarried, had no job, and indeed seemed on the whole to disapprove of people working to maintain what he called the deliquescent putrefaction of Western civilisation. Did this mean that he was a Communist? His cawing laugh was sufficient answer, but then what *was* he?

'I support Michelangelo and Shakespeare, Shelley and Kierkegaard, Blake and Bishop Berkeley. I oppose Voltaire and Diderot . . .'

The list of those he opposed was longer than that of those he supported. He was a bombastic bore. Indeed, Ruthven made up a rhyme which he repeated inexhaustibly afterwards. 'Little Tommy Tucker sang for his supper, but big Tommy Tucker was a boring fucker.' Yet behind the bombast was some sort of pleading.

'When are you going to read my poems?' he demanded at the end of the evening. 'Bastable wrote to you about me, didn't he?' I said yes. 'He thinks I am a poet.' I made no reply to this. Standing outside my cellar entrance, scarecrow body leaning forward, he said, 'Getting printed. That means a lot to me. I must get printed, people must be made to understand.' I said good night, and with a return to his faintly threatening manner, he said he would ring up.

I read the poems that night. They were less clotted with bits of culture than his conversation. There were rambling rhetorical invocations of gods and demons, an ode to 'All Past and Future Saviours', another to 'The Twentieth Century Dead', the style a mixture of Flecker at his most posterishly colourful, Swinburne at his vaguest.

On the following day he rang me at my office and said, 'Well?'

I said something about not liking anything sufficiently, and he cut me short.

'All right. Come to supper. One day next week. Any day, name one.'

I might have said firmly *no, not at any time*, but I have always found that difficult. I named a day, he gave me the address, then slammed down the receiver so that the sound reverberated in my ear. He must immediately have got in touch with Bastable, for a couple of days later I had a note. 'I am sorry that you did not care for Tucker's poems. I think you may be wrong, and that in spite of an occasional wildness of expression and style, he may well be the poet our time is awaiting. In any case he is rather a protégé of mine, and I shall be glad of anything you can do for him.' So far from Bastable getting me any reviewing, it appeared that I was to do him favours.

Tucker lived in a dingy street at the back of King's Cross station. He greeted me eagerly, clasped my hand with both of his. His shirt hung loose outside his trousers in the manner of some modern footballers. The tic beneath his eye twitched, he was excited.

'This is my humble abode.' It was a small room with a table, a couple of chairs, some bookshelves. Two or three dismal daubs were pinned up on the walls. The abode was even humbler than my cellar. 'Here's Deirdre.'

Deirdre was a thin girl with dark lank hair. She wore a slightly dirty blue dress and sandals, and hardly looked at me as she whispered 'Hallo'.

'Got to go round the corner', Tucker said. 'Back shortly. Deirdre will entertain you. She's at the International Arts College. Those are hers.' He gestured at the daubs.

When we were alone Deirdre sat on one hard chair, I on the other. 'Tom's wonderful', she whispered. 'He knows so much. You're going to publish his poems, aren't you? He had one three months ago in *Life and Letters*, and another in the *London Helicon*. He says that's a breakthrough, and it's happened since I came here. To live, I mean.' The whisper sank so low that she was almost inaudible. 'I'm not a Londoner, you know. I come from Welwyn Garden City.'

Feet sounded on the stairs. Tucker returned panting, carrying bottles. He said to Deirdre, 'Glasses. Food.' She got up, went obediently into the next room.

'That's your kitchen?'

He gave his caw. 'And bedroom. Deirdre's a good girl. The life force moves in her.'

Deirdre returned with glasses, plates, cold meat, a bowl of salad. Through the door I glimpsed an unemptied chamber pot. Tucker fetched what looked like a packing case with cloth nailed to the top, sat on that, then filled the glasses.

'I drink to the muses, all nine.'

'I heard from Bastable the other day. How well do you know him?'

'We're in touch.' He took the bowl of salad on to his knee, helped himself liberally, pushed it over to me. 'What do you know about grottoes?'

'Tom knows *all* about them', Deirdre whispered. 'Fascinating.'

Tom certainly knew a great deal about grottoes, and by the end of the evening I knew it too, or might have done if I had not let the knowledge glide gently into one ear and out of the other. He talked about the origins of grottoes in Roman history, their role in Celtic mythology, their links with Welsh bards, the ornamental shellwork in English grottoes of the Middle Ages and its strange similarity to the shellwork in ancient Chinese and Tibetan grottoes, the magical practices enacted in German grottoes . . .

I listened with increasing sullen irritation as Tucker went on and on, with ever more flamboyant gestures, shirt billowing round him, thin arms emerging from its sleeves, the tic working full time. When he had gone down to the lavatory on the half-landing below Deirdre whispered, 'He's a genius. Sometimes I'm really frightened by how much he knows, he's interested in *everything* to do with art.' I should have foreseen, but did not, that on his return Tucker would produce his long poem 'The Grotto' and insist on reading it aloud, arms waving like signals, eyes glaring at me occasionally to see how I was taking it. I took it badly. The tedious poem, Deirdre's worshipfulness, was too much. I stopped him before he had finished, said something to the effect that poems now should be concerned with what went on in the present and not with mythological grottoes, and left.

Deirdre looked puzzled at my departure. Something had gone wrong, but what? Tucker, deflated, accompanied me to my bus. He did not stop talking.

'Poetry must deal with the eternal things, isn't that so? Its ideal is beauty, it aspires to the condition of music.' I got on to my bus. 'Remember Keats. Remember Poe', he shouted after me.

I half-expected another slender sheaf, but none came. A couple of weeks later, however, Bastable telephoned and asked, in his hesitant way, what I had been saying to young Tucker. 'He has – ah – given his adherence to Sir Oswald Mosley.'

'Joined the Fascists, you mean?'

That was what Bastable meant, although he did not like to hear it expressed so baldly. Tucker had said something to him about the redemption of Britain, and spoken of the need for poetry, philosophy and politics to be blended into one. Bastable felt that this was a consequence of something I had said. I denied it.

'Frankly, I think he's half dotty.'

'He is erratic, I agree.' A pause. 'And yet I feel there is something in him, the possibility of greatness.'

I would have agreed that there *was* something in Tucker, some talent struggling to emerge. His relationship with Bastable puzzled me. Ruthven added a couple of lines to his first Tucker couplet which he presented as a solution. It now ran:

> Tommy Tucker's
> A boring fucker.
> But being Bastable's bumboy
> Gives him some joy.

I did not believe this. Ruthven had never met Bastable.

I saw one or two of Tucker's poems in little magazines, full of rhetoric as ever, but now invoking Britain's past greatness and calling for a modern redeemer. Then came Munich, the threat of immediate war, and with the patched-up peace the certainty of a future one. Tucker passed out of my mind.

I saw him for the last time a little more than a year later, in the early days of the War. I had been invited to a party in Chelsea given by a rich young painter named Harry Playner, who said he would like to paint me, an offer I declined when I learned that the portrait would take at least a year. Playner had an up-to-date flat off the King's Road, with Moholy-Nagy photograms on the walls and lots of tubular furniture about. I was sipping a glass of wine and reflecting that I knew nobody, when a voice said 'Hallo.'

It was Deirdre, hardly recognisable with hair piled up on top of her head, and a dress both clean and new. Even her voice had gained in strength. I asked about Tucker.

'Oh, we were washed up months ago. I'm with Harry now.' Welwyn Garden City had clearly been outgrown. 'Tom's here though, the Countess brought him. Have you met her?'

I said I hadn't. The Countess was famous for the number and brevity of her love affairs, all of them conducted in the world of art and letters. She had sprained or broken an ankle and sat on a sofa, one foot up, holding court. She seemed to me a raddled old thing (but I was in my twenties), highly and artificially coloured, with a bulbous nose and liver-spotted hands loaded with rings. (A recent biography called her fascinatingly ugly.) She held out the ringed hand, no doubt to be kissed, but I shook it. Then Deirdre murmured my name, with surprising effect.

'You are *Julian Symons*.' She burst into laughter, apparently irrepressible, while I stood and stared at her. 'Oh, Mr Symons, I am most amused to meet you.'

I backed away. Deirdre stood with her mouth open. Then one of the admirers leaning over the sofa murmured something to the Countess, her attention was distracted, the scene over. Why was I an object of mirth? I had no idea.

A couple of minutes later I was tapped on the shoulder. It was Tucker. He was in the uniform of an infantry regiment, two pips up. Presumably he had been fitted for the uniform, but sleeves and trouser legs were still remarkably short. He saw my surprise.

'I volunteered at once. The only thing to do.'

'I thought your politics –'

'Politics means nothing, poetry means nothing, do you agree? All that's finished. Remember Eluard? "I spit in the face of the despicable man who does not prefer of all my poems this Critique of Poetry". The Critique of Poetry means action. Remember Rimbaud –'

His waving hand knocked two glasses off a passing waiter's tray. He took my jacket between finger and thumb and led me to a corner. Spittle touched my face as he told me that today poetry had *become* action, this was the synthesis Hegel had been looking for and never found, and action itself would be transformed into a national poetry, a Homerian epic of war and liberation. 'When the time for singing comes', he shouted, 'I shall be the singer.'

It took me five minutes to escape from him.

Early in 1940 I had a note in Bastable's neat character-less hand. 'You may be interested to know that Lieutenant Thomas Tucker died last week in France, as the result of a tragic accident. He was in charge of a patrol which strayed over into the French lines, failed to answer when challenged, and was machine gunned, with total loss of life. His poetic talent was great, and those who failed to recognise it have much to answer for. He might have been the poet of an era, but became only the victim of a war.'

This last phrase he repeated when he wrote a paragraph about Tucker's unfulfilled promise in a *causerie*.

The mystery of his interest in Tucker was cleared up when by chance I mentioned Tucker's name to Norris Tibbs, literary editor of the *New Outlook*.

'Bloody pain in the neck, always sending in poems, none of them any good. Much too long for us anyway. His father took me out to lunch once, said what a good poet he was. Took me to the Ritz. Trying to bribe a Socialist with food and drink, can you imagine? Not that good food either.'

'His father?'

'Old what d'ye call 'em, who writes all that piss and wind in *Time and Tide* and the *Spectator*. Bastable.'

'But his mother wasn't Mrs Bastable?'

'Of course not. The old geezer had a rush of blood to the loins when he was young, had an affair with the Countess, lasted long enough to produce TT.'

'Why was he called Tucker?'

'They farmed him out to foster-parents, he took their name. The Countess used to think it was funny, the way Bastable tried to push the boy without ever saying, I'm his dad.' So that was why she had laughed, because Bastable had told her I was a recalcitrant editor. 'Everybody knows the story.'

'I didn't.'

'You're too young', Norris said gloomily.

I never heard from Bastable again. He died in 1947, the book about Henley still not completed.

# Georgie Boy

I FIRST MET Georgie Boy at one of the irregular, but more or less monthly meetings held upstairs in the Salisbury just after the end of World War II. The meetings were run by a group associated with *Our Time*, perhaps the most interesting of the period's Left-wing magazines. At some time during the War it changed from a small propaganda sheet with very limited appeal into something with a larger page size and illustrations, a magazine that especially through its articles on film and theatre anticipated the emphasis later placed on 'popular culture'. Reports came of copies sold in bus garages and at local Labour Party meetings. In that heyday after the War when almost any change in society seemed possible, *Our Time* flourished. The period was brief. Memory tells me that by 1950 *Our Time* had passed, or nearly so.

Those Salisbury evenings were in the flourishing years. The Salisbury was and is an attractive pub in St Martin's Lane. Its scalloped Edwardian seats are backed with red plush, and the interior room also done out in red plush has been called, with more than a touch of exaggeration, an approach to the long-departed Café Royal. Upstairs there were billiard tables, but the baize cloths were covered when we sat or stood around with our pints of beer while some subject relating to the writer, the audience, the social connection between them, was begun by an invited speaker or an *Our Time* editor, and continued as general discussion. The figure I recall most clearly from those evenings is Randall Swingler – Randall Carline Angelus Swingler, as he was named by the Anglican Rural Dean who sired him and six other children. Randall wrote two novels but was not much of a novelist, and some volumes of poetry which never matched his desire to make a large definitive statement about the human condition in his time and place. He was until 1952 a member of the Communist Party, but one who welcomed heretics so warmly that he was suspected by severer Party intellectuals of harbouring heretical thoughts himself. The sweetness of Randall's smile reflected a nature basically uncontentious, and his Communism blended comfortably into bohemianism. When he dropped dead outside the French pub in 1967, the end on the barricades envisioned in his youth was in every sense a long way away.

I was living then at Blackheath in the flat above Roy Fuller, and we sometimes went together to the Salisbury evenings, along with another local poet named Peter Hewitt, and Peter's wife Diana. Among the forty or fifty others I remember the Australian poet John Manifold, Jack Lindsay, who was like Randall one of *Our Time*'s editors, Arnold Rattenbury, and two or three potential commissars who kept watchful eyes and ears open to what went on. And of course George Constant, Georgie Boy.

On the evening I met him the discussion had moved around the shortcomings of other magazines thought to be unprogressive in character, *Horizon* and *Polemic* being prime examples. Randall, as ever, was against condemnation and held up a copy of *Polemic*, praising particularly its abstract cover. What did the *cover* matter, somebody said, when the contents were so thoroughly reactionary? (I forget whether it was before or after this that Randall himself wrote an article in *Polemic* rebutting a piece by George Orwell. Certainly when he did so disapproval was expressed, by some, of his appearance in such a magazine.) The important thing, Randall said, was to avoid sectarianism. There were good things in both magazines, especially *Horizon*. He mentioned the names of Evelyn Waugh and Graham Greene, praising in particular *The Power and the Glory*. Somebody said: 'But doesn't that make it all the worse?', and somebody else laughed. Others laughed too.

The speaker stuck to his point. 'I mean, if he's a good writer but he's got wrong opinions, surely it would be better if he *weren't* a good writer, he'd do less harm.' At that I turned my head, to see the utterer of such confident simplicities. I saw a fair curly-haired ruddy young man, who blushed at finding himself momentarily the centre of attention, and said nothing more.

A couple of weeks later I was in the Chancery Lane office of the *New Outlook*, a Left-wing weekly for which I sometimes reviewed, in search of the literary editor Norris Tibbs. A woman in the outer office, a battered Polish ex-Communist of enchanting ugliness who had abandoned her unpronounceable name and called herself Elsie Smith, said that I would find Norris round the corner as usual, having a liquid lunch in the Plough. A door at the political end of the paper opened – from the little outer office you went one way into politics, the other into literature – and a voice said 'Hallo there'. I had difficulty in placing the smiling face, then recognised it as that of the young man in the Salisbury. 'Going to look for Norris? I'm on my way to the Plough.'

As we walked round he bubbled over with confidences. His name was George Constant, his father was a tram-driver, he was the oldest of three children, he had been a sergeant in the Signals but had refused to allow his name to be sent up for a commission. 'The war was nearly over, and then I didn't want to leave the lads, and I've got no education, I'm bone ignorant.' He was single but thought everybody should get married and have children. 'Kind of shows you believe in the future, know what I mean?' Without a break he went on: 'I liked that review of Turgenev you did a couple of weeks back. Great stuff, real think-piece, wish I could write like that. I can pour out the words, you know, but got nothing up top.' The ingenuous smile that accompanied this remark made him look about eighteen. He was in fact, I learned later, twenty-three.

In the Plough we found Norris, a small dark gloomy man, who only cheered up when expressing disbelief in the possible fruition of his Socialist beliefs. He greeted us with tolerance rather than enthusiasm, accepted another pint of beer, and also expressed approval of the Turgenev article.

'But d'you know what they said?' *They* were the politicos on the other side of the outer office. 'What percentage of our readers had ever heard of Turgenev? How about some pieces on contemporary English writers? I ask you, I just ask you. Trouble with Socialists is they're all Philistines, trouble with people who read intelligent books is they're not Socialists.' This would-be aphorism cheered Norris up momentarily. George Constant saw somebody he knew at the other side of the bar, excused himself. I asked about him.

'Georgie Boy? They took him on from some local paper, supposed to have Party contacts, going to write a column 'Inside Politics', something like that. They say he can write. Trouble is, he doesn't *know* anything.' Lack of this unspecified knowledge was the severest criticism Norris could make.

'He seems pretty naive'.

'Naive! He's bloody ignorant. Mind you, a nice enough lad. That's what's wrong nowadays, they're nice but ignorant.' And Norris was submerged again in the depths of his own knowledge.

A similar view was expressed more enthusiastically by tough old Elsie. 'You knew we call him Georgie Boy? He's so sweet and so *fresh* I want to pat that curly hair every time I see him. He really believes things can be done, problems can be solved, people mean what they say. When I was in the Polish party we always used to disregard what people said and wrote, tried to work everything out in terms of power groups fighting each other. Georgie Boy, the way he looks and the way he thinks, it's refreshing.'

I read the column, which was called 'Insider's View' by George Constant. It was a kind of political gossip column, of a kind familiar now but then unusual, devoted almost entirely to the Labour Party. George's innocence served him well. He made no approach to those at the top of the Government tree – Bevin, Dalton, Cripps, Attlee, Morrison – but talked to junior

Ministers, backbenchers, Zionists and anti-Zionists, pro- and anti-Communist trade union figures. His weekly column was full of plans, possibilities, plots, recounted in a jaunty but sympathetic way. 'Lively laughing Charles Saxton backs instant orange juice for all under fives . . . Kidderminster member Mary Clayton is passionate to get brain-damaging fisticuffs banned . . . eloquent Edgar Enders says let's be rational about Uncle Joe . . .' This kind of thing never looks impressive many years after, but it did seem uncommonly fresh at the time. And if you read Georgie Boy every week you slowly realised that although a hostile word was hardly ever said, the final effect of several reports on the campaign to ban boxing was to make Mary Clayton seem slightly ridiculous. There was never a sharp word but often a snide reference, about such things as the junior Minister who often preached economy but always travelled in a railway carriage reserved for his personal use. Altogether, the column was a success.

For some reason Georgie liked me, or at any rate liked talking to me. His attendance at the Salisbury had been fortuitous, for his interest in literature was slight and he had come along in the hope of finding something worth reporting. But he was aware that he should know something about the right books, and took me as a kind of guide. After the Turgenev piece I had retrieved myself with an article about American proletarian novelists from Charles Norris to Nelson Algren and James T. Farrell, and another about committed writers, commitment being a fashionable word of the time. *They* had been generally approving, although deprecating what was discovered to be a negative tone. Georgie was full of enthusiasm.

'Terrific, Julian, a real think-piece. Look, would you do something for me? Make out a list of stuff I should read, I don't mean Tolstoy and all that, but modern stuff. Books that have got social comment, what you call commitment. I'll never set up my stall as a critic, but at least I'll know a bit what I'm talking about.' This was accompanied by his shy engaging smile. I made out a list of twenty books, from

*The Ragged-Trousered Philanthropists* to *A World I Never Made*, but don't know how many of them he read. A couple of weeks later he rang me urgently for advice. He had been invited to a wedding, and was expected to wear a morning coat and striped trousers. Would it be a betrayal of Socialist principles to put on such clothes? No, I said, of course not.

'But it's a sort of uniform, isn't that right? Class differentiation, I don't see how you can call it anything else. My dad's never worn stuff like that in his life, wouldn't know what it was. I had to ask to find out.'

'If you feel that strongly, say no. But remember Attlee and Bevin and the others dress up when they have to.'

'Are they Socialists, though? If they are, shouldn't they have held out against class dress? But still, you think it's all right?'

'Why don't you ask *them?*' I referred to the paper's politicos.

'I have. They just think it's a joke. All right then, I'll go to Mossbross.'

Afterwards he was tellingly articulate – Georgie Boy was never less than articulate – about the occasion to Elsie and myself.

'Honestly it was awful. I mean, how stuffed can a stuffed shirt get? Can you imagine, it was a *Labour* wedding, bride and groom, best man, everybody, a couple of Ministers too – and what sort of show did we put on? If people go on like that, it's a joke to talk about Socialist Britain.'

'You're right, Georgie Boy'. Elsie's broad battered face rarely reflected emotion, but I could tell that she was moved. 'In Poland, Germany, France, all over Europe, revolutionary Socialists think the only important thing is theory, if it's according to Marx it's kosher, and if you've got the theory right it doesn't matter how badly you behave, who you betray.' I knew her own past had been stormy, two marriages to Party functionaries, time spent in a Polish prison. 'But it isn't so.'

'Elsie, we're talking about respectable middle-class Englishmen, not revolutionary Middle Europeans, and they're just obeying social custom, not betraying anybody.'

'It matters', Elsie said decisively. Georgie had been looking from one of us to the other. Now he nodded agreement with Elsie.

A couple of weeks later I met him in the street – I had just come out of a cinema, he had been at a Hands Off Israel meeting which he was reporting for the paper – and he invited me to come back for supper and meet his parents. Wouldn't an unexpected guest be a problem, I asked (rationing was still severe)? Georgie gave me his confident confiding smile, and said it was all right, people often dropped in. He was quite right, for the big bowl of thick soupish stew fed seven of us, the senior Constants, Georgie's two younger brothers, and a friend of his father from the local union branch. Mrs Constant was a kind of archetypal working-class mother, concerned chiefly to see that everybody had enough to eat, but Charles Constant was a formidable figure. The large nose looked as if it had been cut out of rock, the chin was a rocky peak, deep-set grey eyes looked hard at you. He spoke little but decisively, whether it was to say that the youngest boy Tommy had had enough to eat, or that Ernest Bevin was a traitor to the British working class. In the parlour where we ate there were photographs on the wall of great occasions in the Labour movement, trams immobilised at New Cross during the General Strike, Durham miners' rallies, a sea of faces at a Glasgow strike meeting in 1919. There were photographs also of Keir Hardie, George Lansbury, A. J. Cook, none of Ramsay MacDonald or Attlee. It was easy to see that any dissent from a radical viewpoint would get short shrift here.

Charles Constant hardly spoke to me during supper, but afterwards said: 'Georgie's talked about you, a real writer he says you are. And what's the purpose of it?' He did not wait for a reply. 'I'll tell you what it should be. To make a better society, even things out, give everyone a chance. Georgie here now, do you suppose he wouldn't have been good enough for Oxford if he'd had the chance?' I said I hadn't been to university myself. 'Is that right? Money I suppose, it all comes down to money. Destroy privilege, lad, that's the job ahead for the Labour movement.'

'And they're not doing it', his friend said.

Georgie protested. 'Give them a chance. A lot of things have changed. And they've only been in just over three years.'

The searchlight of Mr Constant's grey eyes was directed on his son. '*Only*, did you say only? They've had time to change society, you can do it in three months if you've got the will, let alone three years. And what have they done? A little bit here, a bit there, nibbling the edges. And how about your man Bevan, who's supposed to be so radical, what's he doing? Drinking in clubs with the class enemy, you'd not have found Arthur Cook doing that. You can write what you like in your paper about prospects for the future, there won't be another chance to change things, I tell you that.'

'Now dad, I'm sure Georgie's doing his best', his wife said. She did not mention me. 'There's no call to go on like that.'

'I've done.' He waved a big hand. 'Said my piece. No offence meant to anybody, nothing personal.'

Georgie saw me back to the bus stop for Blackheath. He was even more voluble than usual. 'Dad's a wonderful man, been in the movement since he was fourteen, but he's stuck back in the Twenties and Thirties, doesn't realise there's no need to man the barricades any more, we're in control. Like Hartley Shawcross said, we're the masters now. Trouble with dad is he wants everything to have happened yesterday. He'd like to wipe out the War, forget all about it, get back to the class struggle, but that's not the way things are. You can't wipe out the war, it changed everything, right?'

'Yes', I said. 'You can't wipe out the war.'

In the next two or three months I was busy working on a crime story and making a selection from Samuel Johnson for a now defunct firm called the Falcon Press, and as always when busy with other things I abjured reviewing. It wasn't until I saw Elsie at a BBC party that I heard what had been happening at the *New Outlook*. When I asked about the paper, she made a face.

'You hadn't heard? I'm not there any more.' I was surprised. There were few people who knew more than Elsie about the intricacies of European radical politics or had met more of the people involved in them, and I'd always thought of her as a fixture. I asked why she'd left.

'Not exactly left. VR decided that we didn't need all those long articles about politics inside Yugoslavia and the way Togliatti and Nenni are manoeuvring in Italy.' VR was the editor and chief politico, a man said to be on first name terms with every important Minister. 'More about Britain, less about Europe is the policy, so goodbye Elsie. What does she know about Britain, except that she's lived here ten years?' Her smile was painful. 'No need to worry, Elsie has been taken to the wide bosom of the BBC Foreign Service. I miss the paper though.'

I asked about Georgie Boy, and she said he had been made a deputy editor. That had been Elsie's own position. 'You mean he's replaced you?'

'You mustn't jump to conclusions, Georgie Boy told me so himself. With a smile so sweet I still wanted to pat him on the head. Very likely it would have happened whether he'd been there or not. Still, maybe Lenin was right, we should be careful about patting people on the head.'

But could the two things possibly be unconnected? At least the shift in policy had been very handy for Georgie, who knew next to nothing about Europe. 'It's their loss.'

'You don't have to say nice things to an old woman.' Her wide grin with its display of crooked teeth seemed more genuine this time.

The next I heard of Georgie was from Norris Tibbs, when I emerged from seclusion and went in search of books for review. Norris was in his office for once, picking his teeth while correcting galleys. He steered me in the direction of books I didn't want, but in the end reluctantly agreed to give me Graham Greene's *The Heart of the Matter*, and we adjourned to the Plough. When I asked how the paper was going, he shook his head.

'Nothing but trouble, interference all the time. Shouldn't be surprised if they said I'd given too much space to *that*.' He jerked a thumb at the Graham Greene novel. 'Made the main feature a book about Coleridge last week. They asked whether I couldn't have found something by a living author for the lead. How many Yorkshire miners read Coleridge?' He gave a martyred laugh.

I remembered the remark about Graham Greene at the Salisbury. 'Does Georgie interfere?'

'Georgie? He's gone to the Beaver, and so has Osbert. I thought you'd know.'

Delighted to find somebody ignorant of current gossip, he proceeded to tell me. Osbert Winkle was the paper's theatre critic, a bright young man like Georgie, but unlike him one just down from Oxford. The Beaver (at this distance of time it had better be said that this was the Canadian newspaper tycoon Lord Beaverbrook) regarded papers like the *New Outlook* as breeding grounds for recruits to his empire. Georgie Boy and Osbert Winkle had been separately summoned to dinner, separately wooed. Osbert had succumbed immediately, Georgie Boy had said no, and returned breathing loyalty to VR. Then the Beaver had upped his offer, and Georgie had changed his mind. Osbert had just been installed as drama critic on a Beaverbrook paper.

Norris told me all this with many a meaningful nudge and unspoken *I told you so*. Goodbye Georgie Boy, I thought, and was surprised when he rang me up shortly afterwards and asked me to lunch. We ate in an expensive chop house off Fleet Street, and Georgie's usual sports jacket and trousers had been replaced by a smart suit. He gave me a minute by minute account of the evening with the Beaver.

'He's a real horror, no doubt about that, but you can't help liking him. I mean, Michael liked him.' Michael Foot had edited the *Evening Standard* for a while during the War. 'Do you know what he said to me about Osbert? "You know why I want that young man? He's got a black soul. A drama critic should have a black soul." I wonder what he said to Osbert about me?'

'I wonder.'

Georgie put down his knife and fork, which he still used in the pick-and-shovel manner of his father. 'I know what you're thinking, Julian, he's sold out. But what would you have done?'

'Said yes, very likely. I've never had the chance, never been tempted.'

'Be serious.' His own face positively shone with seriousness, from gleaming curls to mobile chin. 'You know I'm a Socialist, I said to the old man, anything I write will be from that point of view. That's just why I want you, my boy, he said. No censorship? I asked, and he said: "Do you ever find Low not saying what he pleases?"' (David Low had been the *Evening Standard* cartoonist for years.) 'Let's face it, I'll be talking to a million people instead of thirty thousand. Can you tell me that isn't a good thing?'

'What does your father think?'

I got the confiding Georgie Boy smile. 'I love dad, but I've told you he belongs to the past, we don't live in his world any more.' When we parted he said, 'I was pretty raw when we met, and I'm not the greatest brain in the world, I know that. Think-pieces, they're beyond me, I'm just a journalist and a Socialist. I wanted you to know I haven't changed my opinions, never will.'

I read some of the articles he wrote, about plans for the development of London, divisions in the Tory party, Labour's way ahead. Now that he'd moved up in the world there were quite a lot of interviews with Ministers. There seemed a sense of constraint about most of the articles, as though he was a boxer not punching his weight, and it seemed to me that the tone changed with the political climate. When the Tories took office in 1951 his name ceased to appear on the features page. Osbert Winkle had already departed for one of the classy Sundays. Had Georgie done the same? Norris told me that he was still with the Beaver, but had moved over to an administrative job.

A year later I received an invitation to his wedding reception. The bride was an American girl named Lillian Montgomery, said to be connected in some way with Montgomery Ward, and certainly not short of the ready. The reception was at the Savoy, champagne flowed, there was a splendid buffet. The bride's father, a squarehead with cropped hair and rimless spectacles, made a speech about his lovely little girl. The best man, an adjutant of the Beaver named Sir William Something, made a speech saying Georgie had always been up-and-coming but now he'd arrived. Lillian giggled when I kissed her cheek, but she had giggled during the speeches, so why should she stop when I kissed her? Georgie, extremely handsome in his morning coat, clasped my hand in both his own and said it was wonderful to see me.

There was a call for Mr Constant to say something, and he was pushed or dragged forward. He looked awkward in what was obviously a little-worn suit with its stiff white collar, awkward and somehow smaller, as though the surroundings and the company had diminished him. 'Come on, dad, say something', his wife cried. Georgie echoed his mother, just a little nervously. There was a hush when he stood with a space cleared round him, the big nose turning from side to side as though sniffing out enemies.

'Not much to say. Georgie's always been a good lad, we've been proud of him, hope we always shall be.' A pause. 'Wish him and Lillian the best of luck. Where he works, he'll need it.'

There was the briefest silence, then Georgie roared with laughter, clapped his father's shoulder, said good old dad. Lillian went on giggling.

They settled down in a house in the Boltons, bought by Mr Montgomery. In five years Lillian produced three children. Were they gigglers like their mother, or smilers like their father? I cannot say, for I have never met them.

The rest of Georgie's story belongs in part to the ever-varying yet always remarkably similar legends of Fleet Street, in part to the History of Consensus Man. I had no personal part in it, even as a witness. His rise in the newspaper world was rocketlike, his fall suitably abrupt. He was assistant editor of this, deputy chief editor of that, renowned as an administrative cost-cutter. That phase of his career reached its apogee with a top administrative appointment in which he sacked people wholesale in the name of economy. 'There's too much fat on the papers', he was quoted as saying. 'I'm cutting it away, preserving a healthy body and a strong heart.' When he dismissed his former best man Sir William Something, however, there was a cry of enough. Georgie Boy got a handsome handout and his marching orders.

But he was still a young man, and his administrative talent had been spotted. In the Sixties and Seventies he became first a director, then the chief executive, of a large building consortium. His personal friendship with many Labour politicians was immensely helpful during the fifteen years when, with the short Heathian interregnum, the party was in power. His activities flowed out from business to the arts and sciences. He was chairman of several committees, sat on others, was a member of many quangos. I saw him occasionally at the Gay Hussar at lunch with Labour politicians, and was always greeted by the friendliest wave, or if he paused to say hallo with the warmest two-handed greeting.

Of these occasions I remember clearly only one, when I had been invited as a guest to an Institute of Directors meeting which was said to be discussing business aid for the arts. There proved to be general directorial agreement that the arts should receive support only if business men could look for tax concessions, or some positive cash return on their money. Georgie spoke eloquently in favour of the tax concessions which no government has yet approved. By his side on the platform were men who looked like George Grosz caricatures of profiteers, and hard-faced young bankers wearing Turnbull and Asser shirts who listened distrustfully to every word he said. Afterwards I said something about the company he kept. He nodded, but not in agreement. 'I know

31

how they look. Trouble is, Julian, you don't know them, don't know what they're really like. The more you see of them the more you realise they're friendly, democratic, just so damned *nice*.'

Georgie Boy became Sir George Constant in the middle Seventies, in Harold Wilson's last government. *The Times* carried a picture of him outside the Palace, erect, handsome and, naturally enough, smiling.

# Ella, a success story

I FIRST KNEW Ella because my sister played the piano, singing to her own accompaniment. She sang the Indian Love Lyrics and other songs of unfulfilled or unrequited love:

> Long years ago, in old Madrid,
> Where softly sighed of love the light guitar,
> Two sparkling eyes a lattice hid,
> Two eyes as darkly bright as love's own star.

My mother was enchanted. She was determined that one of her sons also should be in some way musical, and the choice fell on me as the youngest. For a year I was taught the violin, for several more the piano. In musical theory my progress was not spectacular but good. I learned to read music, passed an examination, received a certificate. Practice, fingers striking the keys, was another matter. I quickly managed a spirited rendering of the 'Marseillaise', but got no further. My mother spent hours listening to me play chords over and over, varying them with gruesomely inaccurate renderings of some of the other simple pieces taught me by Mrs O'Reilly. When I was fourteen she reluctantly gave nature best, and I scraped all traces of musical knowledge from my mind. Today I could not find middle C on the piano, although I still feel the verbal fascination of terms like crotchet and quaver. What is a quaver? Half a crotchet. And what then of the delicious, near-magical demi-semi-quaver . . . ?

Mrs O'Reilly was a plump smiling Irishwoman, and I went

twice a week for music lessons to her house in Rush Hill Road, off Lavender Hill. The practice lesson I attended on my own, but theory was taken by the whole class of seven or eight, only two of them boys, sitting round Mrs O'Reilly's dining table. In my last couple of years these sessions were enlivened by Jessie Noakes, a late member of the class and the oldest of the group, who played footsie with me under the table. Rush Hill Road is a cul-de-sac with St Matthew's Church at the top of it, and when class was over three or four of us would swing on the wicket gate leading through the churchyard to Gowrie Road, talking and joking, and telling what at the time passed for dirty stories. Jessie was provocative, and kicked up her legs to show her knickers. She had a watch, and when asked the time would giggle and say 'Half past kissing time'. Sometimes we played touch, running through the churchyard into Gowrie and back, and there was also a kind of hide and seek in which a certain spot in the churchyard was home. Jessie always took care to be caught or to catch, guiding a hand to her breasts or slipping her own hand down for a quick exciting fumble at genitals. The other girls had no objection to being held, but were less free with their hands. Lou Verney and I, the two boys, speculated endlessly on the question: would Jessie go on Clapham Common, and if she went, would she do it? The answers proved to be yes, and no.

From such activities Ella, whose name was Brown, stayed rather disdainfully clear. She and one of the other girls always went straight home after class. Ella was a year younger than me, had red hair worn in pigtails, and was called Carrots accordingly. She lived in Nansen, the next road to Gowrie, and said that her father, some sort of minor official at Battersea Town Hall, didn't like her to be out playing on the streets. Jessie mocked her: 'Run along home, Carrots, daddy's waiting'. Ella, books under arm, head down, scurried away.

I first became aware of Ella, as distinct from knowing who she was, when my elementary school, along with the adjoining girls' school, put on a much abbreviated performance of *The Merchant of Venice*, in which I played Shylock and Ella was

34

Portia. My then prevailing stammer vanished when I was on the stage, and she remarked on this.

'Do you like acting? I might be an actress.' I don't know what reply I made, probably a stammering one, because she said 'Why don't you stutter when you're being Shylock? You don't sound anything like so silly when you don't stutter, you should try and get out of it.' Without telling her that I had taken more than one cure with no effect, I said it was not so easy. 'Of course it is. You can do anything if you really want to. Are you going to be an ordinary person? I'm not. I've got brains, my dad says so.'

I daresay I was impressed by this, because of my own entire uncertainty about what I wanted to do or be. Depression was in the air, and I suppose my feeling was that if you had a job you'd be wise to hang on to it, whether you had brains or not.

The next time I saw her was some years later, in the rather surprising context of one of the home matches played by our old boys' cricket team, although 'home' meant merely a pitch hired by us at Motspur Park. She was brought along by Dick Stansted, our opening batsman, a rather tough little fellow who worked as an apprentice printer on a local newspaper. I asked what she was doing, and she said she was an assistant at Cooper and Lucas, a firm in the district that sold artists' materials.

'I thought you were going to be somebody, not just an ordinary person.'

She had the very white skin that often goes with red hair, and now she blushed. 'I'm not, don't worry. What are *you* doing?' She laughed when I said I was a shorthand typist in an engineering company. 'And you waste your time playing with this lot. At least you're the captain, I suppose that's something.'

In spite of the comment about *this lot* she paid attention to the cricket, and for the rest of the season was a regular attendant. She wasn't particularly liked by the other girls, who used words like standoffish or toffee-nosed about her.

35

To me her attitude was one of faint contempt with a slight admixture of respect. On the one hand I was a shorthand typist, and so obviously very ordinary. On the other, I was the captain of a team in which I had no proper place on the ground of cricketing merit, and she respected that as a kind of successful con trick. She also used an occasional phrase or two about books and authors, to show the others that the two of us were in a class apart. She was reading Galsworthy and Bennett, while I was occupied with Joyce and Wyndham Lewis, so that from my point of view she was hardly up-to-date. Then she discovered women writers, Virginia Woolf and Katherine Mansfield, and annoyed everybody by reading *The Voyage Out* through most of one match.

She didn't seem particularly keen on Dick Stansted, but he was mad about her. Dick had a Harley Davidson motorbike plus sidecar, and she usually went off in the sidecar as soon as a match was over, without taking part in the team's ritual booze-up. When she missed a match through having 'flu, Dick talked to me about her.

'She's a wonderful girl, you know. Very high powered.'

'Dick, she's a shop assistant.'

He shook his head. 'You don't know her like I do. Did she tell you she'd been taking evening class courses for the last two years? Journalism and French, then this year she took German. She thinks a lot of you.'

I said she took care not to show it.

Perhaps I should describe Ella as she was at the time, in her early twenties. She had strong features, a face rather large and long, slightly equine. Very white complexion. Breasts distinctly present without making themselves conspicuous, good figure, but thickish legs and rather large feet. Expression slightly sceptical, as though prepared to disbelieve on principle anything you said to her, mouth uncommonly firm. The expression and the mouth she got from her father. I saw them once together in the street, and said hallo. He looked as if I were a bad herring dangled under his nose, and I thought his lips were glued together until he opened his mouth to say

Ella had mentioned me, and showed a double row of very white false choppers.

But I have not mentioned woman's crowning glory: Ella's hair, which was no longer in pigtails but piled on top of her head in a manner unquestionably striking. *Carroty* as a descriptive term would now certainly have been replaced by the more acceptable *auburn*. Ella could not possibly have been called a beautiful woman, and my belief is that the many men who later found her attractive (I even heard her called fascinating) were spellbound by the remarkable thatch which at different periods she wore piled up on top, in great coils round her ears, flowing loose down her back like (as one unkind friend said) a bloody flux, in a page-boy bob, and even ruthlessly cut short, an effect which made her look distinctly masculine. But this variety of hair-dos, rather like the different stylistic approaches made by an artist to his subject, came later. In the Thirties Ella wore her hair piled on top.

After that one season Ella came to very few matches, and in the following year Dick Stansted played only occasionally. Then he gave up altogether. I heard that he had served his apprenticeship and got a job as compositor on the *Daily Express*, that Ella was on the paper too as a sub, or some other lowly position that was still better than being behind the counter at Cooper and Lucas, and that they were married. I was not invited to the wedding, nor was there any reason why I should have been, and I saw nothing of them. I gave up cricket, like Dick. The war came. Ella Brown, now Ella Stansted, passed out of my mind.

In 1944 I was invalided out of the Army and looked around for a congenial job, which proved surprisingly difficult to find. (At least, I was surprised.) I ended up as a copywriter in an advertising agency, but before I got that job I was interviewed by a bulky pipe-smoking man at the BBC, whose name I never caught, for a position in what I believe was called Drama and Features. I spent an agreeable half-hour with the pipe-smoker, swopping stories about people we knew, Dylan Thomas, Ruthven Todd and others, but at the end of the half-hour we agreed that I had no qualifications for a job in Drama and Features. No doubt I had not helped my cause by answering a question about what kind of script writing interested me particularly, by replying: 'Well, none of them particularly'. On the way out, trudging gloomily down one of those endless passages that make it possible to confuse BBC buildings with the London Underground, I saw approaching me a red head. It was Ella. She assumed that I was now in the BBC. I could not bring myself to admit that I had been turned down, but said I had been for an interview with Drama and Features.

'Hopeless', she said briskly. 'They'll never get anyone else on establishment. I'm in the French section. No vacancies there, though, full up with Gaullists, I'm the token Englishwoman. Got any German or Italian? No? Pity, I might have been able to help if you had any languages.'

The thought of Ella helping me was somehow not congenial. I said I would manage, and asked about Dick.

'That was a mistake. Didn't take. Dick is – well, just stuck in a rut, happy where he is, reserved occupation and so on. He'll never *do* anything.'

It struck me that Ella would probably say I was not *doing* anything if our conversation continued. I got away before she could say I should attend evening classes.

I stayed in the advertising job more than three years, but only a single incident in my advertising career is relevant to Ella. Our creative director John Nicholas was much in favour of what even then was an old-fashioned approach to advertising. A capable imitative artist himself, Nick was very keen on advertising illustrations that had what he called the lusty music of humanity. He liked advertisements full of people doing things, huge offices full of busy workers, farmers leaning over fences and chatting, a sweating auctioneer with

38

hammer raised about to knock down some priceless article. All these themes Nick worked into advertisements, along with many slices of photographic realism that would have pleased 'Bubbles' Millais or Frith. He detested the use of abstract or near-abstract designs on the lines of McKnight Kauffer or Abram Games, which in those immediate post-war days were becoming fashionable, and his particular aversion was the work of an artist named Antonio Varadi, who signed his posters 'Antonio'. I remember one typical Antonio poster that caused a stir (among advertising people, that is) at the time. It was for a new washing powder named Glo, and the poster consisted of a dazzling pattern of diagonal coloured stripes, of the kind later developed by Bridget Riley, with the word Glo in small capitals at one corner, and in another corner 'Cleanest' in equally small capitals. A thick diagonal shaft led from corner to corner. The ad, adapted from poster to newspaper use, infuriated Nick. He would thump his table and say, 'A lot of lines going this way and that, how does it *sell* the product, I ask you?' He was further infuriated by a series of aphorisms written by Varadi, which received much attention in what passed for the intellectual end of the advertising business. 'The artist who creates an advertisement is not a salesman but a designer' was one, 'The advertisement must first draw attention to itself, only second to its subject' another, 'Art to touch the heart is designed in the mind' a third. Piss and wind, Nick said, piss and wind. And what kind of name was Antonio Varadi? Nick went around singing 'Hey ho, Antonio, with his ice cream cart', and labelled Varadi the ice cream merchant.

It can be imagined, then, that when we obtained an account that was to be handled in collaboration with Varadi's much bigger agency, so that Nick would have to work personally with the ice cream merchant, his pleasure was not unalloyed. When Varadi invited him to dinner Nick flinched at the prospect, and asked me to go along with him. I knew all about modern art, or at least could tell a Mondrian from a Ben Nicholson, whereas to Nick both looked as if they had been put together by somebody playing with kids' building blocks. Would Mr Varadi mind if Mr Nicholas brought along a creative man who was really tuned in to modern art? Mr Varadi – 'my name is Tony' – would be delighted.

Varadi lived in a small block of flats off Lowndes Square. There was a doorman in the hall, the lift interior had imitation marbling, unusual things in those austere post-war days. 'Money, boy, I smell money', Nick said as we went up, shaking his head in deprecation of the fact that it should be sticking to the fingers of an ice cream merchant.

Such feelings could not survive long in Varadi's presence. If Nick was a rough Welsh charmer, Varadi was a smooth central European one. He won Nick's heart almost instantly by awareness of paintings Nick had shown in the Royal Academy that year, saying they stood out from most of the pictures like roses among cabbages. Over a glass of champagne he toasted the collaboration. 'I am a tradesman who tries to be an artist', he said. 'You are an artist compelled to be a tradesman'. That was going it a bit, I thought, but Nick looked like a dog praised for bringing back a stick. If you are going to flatter it is hardly possible to spread the butter too thick. From then on it was Nick and Tony.

Because this was a business occasion, Tony said, he had asked no other guests. His wife would be with us in a moment. 'Ah, here she is. Eva, this is John Nicholas, whose paintings you will know. And Julian Symons.'

It was (you will have guessed) Ella. But an Ella looking, it must be said, rather splendid in an off-the-shoulder dark green dress, a heavy gold chain round her neck, gold earrings, and that red hair blazing away on top of her head. Nick, always one to admire flamboyance, and not to be outdone in politeness by any ice cream man however charming, kissed her hands. I shook hands, and we agreed we had met before.

The evening went well. Nick and Tony got on splendidly, and my dubious expertise in relation to abstract art was not tested. Eva/Ella and I made conversation about this and that, without mentioning Mrs O'Reilly or Nansen Road. The next morning, in the office, Nick was exultant.

'We got through it, boy, we went through the baptism of fire and emerged unscathed. I don't take back a word of what I've said about Tony, mind you, but I'll say this, he's a clever fellow, and when you put all the flummery aside he's got his feet on the ground. A tradesman trying to be an artist he called himself, I liked that. And Eva now, what a magnificent woman, a Titian goddess. Did you say you knew her?'

I said we had met when I was trying to get a job in the BBC, and Nick asked nothing more. He was not much interested in other people's lives.

I was surprised when, that afternoon, the telephone rang and a voice said, 'This is Eva. Are you free to have lunch with me one day next week?'

I wondered what could be the object of the invitation, for I did not doubt it had a purpose. I was not under the impression that Eva had any personal interest in me.

At lunch she wore a severe grey suit with a white collar. Was it Varadi's influence that had improved her clothes sense, and where had she got the clothing coupons? She checked me when, by mistake, I called her Ella.

'It's Eva now. Ella was a hopeless name. You changed your name too, remember? When I first knew you it was Gus. That was hopeless too. Where do you live?'

Blackheath, I said. She shook her head.

'Blackheath is no good. The only places to live are in central London or right outside. Chelsea, Fulham, St John's Wood, they're as far out as you should go. Perhaps Hampstead may be possible, a special case. Anywhere else—' She dismissed all the other places.

It was when she said this that I noticed the change in her voice. People talk about a South London accent. I don't believe such an accent exists, but Eva's early companions had been, like mine, mostly the lower middle class girls and boys of Battersea and Clapham, and there *is* a tone,

41

a way of enunciating words, even a set of phrases, that is particular to the area, and wouldn't be quite the same in North London. (I am speaking of the past, obviously. Most of these differences and distinctions have been ironed out today.) Ella would never have said and repeated 'hopeless' as Eva did, nor would she have used a phrase like 'the only places to live'. Had she taken elocution lessons? Possibly, but Eva was a woman who quickly learned the right way to say things, as well as the right things to say.

But what did she want of me? We ran through matters that I felt did not much interest her, whether I liked advertising, had plans for the future, thought of reviving the verse magazine I had run before the war. My replies were mostly negative. Then she got down to cases.

'You still do some reviewing. I see your name occasionally.' She spoke as if reviewing was my last link with civilised life. 'And you've had a couple of detective stories published.' I admitted it. A pause. 'I've written a novel.'

My God, I thought, she wants me to read the manuscript, make suggestions, help to get it published. I hurriedly mentioned my agent's name, offered an introduction. My conjectures were quite wrong. She brushed aside the suggestion.

'It's been accepted, of course.' That *of course* was typical of her. She named the publisher, who was *of course* fashionable. 'But they don't seem prepared or able to put much weight behind it. The thing is—'

'Yes?'

'How do you arrange to get a good window display in Hatchard's? And other bookshops? And reviews, how do you get proper long reviews? There must be a way. What do you do? Ring up the literary editors and ask them out to lunch?'

I stared at her, hardly able to believe what she was saying. Plainly there were things Eva hadn't learned. I began to talk about publishers' publicity departments. She cut me short.

'That's all run of the mill, I've been told all that. I

don't want my book thrown in with the rest of them. It should receive special treatment. How do I get it?'

Stung, I said, 'You don't.' I told her how unlikely it was that a first novel would get a window display in any but a local bookshop, that any approach to literary editors of the kind she had in mind was likely to be counter-productive. She listened, but I doubt if she believed me. At the end I said perhaps Tony could help. She scorned the idea.

'Tony is just—' I thought she was going to say 'hopeless' but she didn't. 'Tony's a phoney. He believes most of the things he says, mind, that's what makes him a phoney. I don't say he's untalented. He's done a very good jacket for the book, and he's publicised himself cleverly, but really he's one of nature's phoneys. He only wants me around to play hostess at dinners and parties.'

'It was your body he was after, your hair especially, not your mind.'

Her pale blue eyes stared at me. 'That's not even faintly funny.'

She had met him at a party given by somebody in the French section at the BBC. I gathered she had been impressed by him, although she was unwilling to admit it. 'And I wasn't going to stay in the BBC for ever, no point in that.' They had been married now for eighteen months, and in material terms she had everything she needed, a good address, decent clothes, money. 'But I don't know, I don't know. We'll see what happens when my book's out.'

What happened to *No Villain Need Be* was what happens to ninety-nine novels in every hundred. It was reviewed here, ignored there, sold its thousand or fifteen hundred copies, most of them to libraries, then sank without trace. Eva didn't send me a copy, feeling perhaps that she had not got value for money from the lunch, and I felt no inclination to buy one. I dipped into it several times in Hatchards (where there was no window display), almost to the point of making it secondhand, but can't now remember anything of the plot, or even the name of a character. Within a few months of its publication Eva and

43

Tony had parted, the brief love-in between Nick and Varadi had ended, our agency had lost the account, and Varadi had been transformed in Nick's eyes from a mere harmless ice cream merchant into an emblem of the corruption of modern art. All this, however, I heard at secondhand, for I had left the agency, and with George Orwell's help (something I have described elsewhere) launched myself uncertainly into free-lance literary life.

I didn't see Eva again for several years, although I came across her name occasionally. Sitting in a doctor's or dentist's waiting room, leafing through one of the smart magazines I never ordinarily read, I would come across articles by Eva Varadi, letters from Berlin or New York, gossipy pieces about who had won which French literary prizes that year, interviews with Salinger, Truman Capote, Paul Bowles. She translated a German novel, and reviewers called the translation sympathetic, lucid, intelligent, the kind of words they often use when ignorant of the original language. She had, it appeared to me, moved out of my literary goldfish bowl into a bigger pool warmed by the sun of money. Then one day I had a call from H'mchoke.

H'mchoke is one of the very few rich people I know, and that of course is not his name. He was given it because the way in which he expressed interest, pleasure or amusement was to utter an interrogative 'H'm?' accompanied by a choking sound which might be called a strangled laugh. Thus H'mchoke might say in an art gallery, 'Rather jolly pictures, h'm?' (choke). The h'm would be on a rising note, and always had a questioning sound, for H'mchoke had no assured opinions about anything. He was South African, perhaps Jewish or Arab, certainly semitically swarthy. His money was rumoured to come from gold or diamond mines, said by some (although of course nobody really knew) to be among the most harshly administered in South Africa. H'mchoke himself was a soft touch in most ways, contributing large sums to relief funds for this and that, putting money into a chain of craft shops, backing an art gallery devoted to British Victorian artists,

44

acting as financial angel for several shows at little theatres.

All of these ventures either failed, or H'mchoke withdrew support from them and so stifled them soon after birth. Although, or perhaps because, he had no real artistic opinions, he was capable of being fired with enthusiasm for almost anything. The True Victorian Gallery might have been successful given a few years to develop and encourage a taste for minor Victorian painters, but H'mchoke, who at the opening show of Highland deer and scenes of family delight or anguish, had gone round saying: 'All very – h'm (choke) – amusing and interesting and perhaps really important, don't you think?', soon felt that 'A Father's Sorrow' and 'A Hero of the Glen' could not easily be made the right fashionable thing, closed the gallery, and was left with dozens of huge canvases on his hands. The man put in to run British Crafts proved to be a crook, who left hurriedly for Brazil after piling up debts of fifty thousand pounds, a small poetry press failed because H'mchoke withdrew support when told that the press was publishing quite the wrong people.

The theatre ventures were mostly connected with H'mchoke's girls. He had girls as some people have colds, three or four times a year, most of them young, without money, and tending not to be house trained – that is, they bathed and washed rarely, and had no idea of how to cook or look after an apartment. All had artistic aspirations, as actresses, poets, novelists, painters, and for the duration of the affair H'mchoke indulged their fantasies. Then Eileen or Anna or Cordelia would disappear, and if she were mentioned H'mchoke would say, 'Just too much, dear boy, simply couldn't do with her. Artistic temperament's all very well, but when it comes to having no idea of personal hygiene it's a little – h'm (choke) – don't you think?'

I was not much excited when H'mchoke said he had a project in mind which might interest me, for I had long ago decided that he had really nothing to recommend him but his money. But still, I went to lunch. We ate at a vegetarian restaurant, and when H'mchoke looked at the menu and said the prices were appalling, my spirits sank. As is not uncommon, H'mchoke's wide generosity was combined with streaks of personal meanness. He always travelled by bus or Underground and refused to use taxis, on the ground that one should support public transport services. He left paying bills until he received the final demand, and was likely to say when one paid him a visit, 'Not much gin left, I'm afraid', triumphantly holding up a bottle with a mere trace of colourless liquid at the bottom, when one felt that a full bottle was stashed away in a cupboard. We drank carrot juice and ate mock beef ragout, while H'mchoke talked about rising prices and falling stocks. In the end I asked why he wanted to see me.

H'mchoke did not care for such directness. He pushed a bit of cabbage round on his plate, then said, 'What do you think of another time? Or to-day and tomorrow?' He gave a couple of h'mchokes at my look of incomprehension. 'Titles. For a new magazine. Feel we need one, don't you? Express the feeling of the time, catch a mandrake root, what the age demands, all that.' He looked at me slyly from the corners of flesh-enfolded small eyes, to see if I had caught the Donne and Pound references.

'Not much. Of the titles, I mean.'

'What about *Vista*?'

I shuddered. 'Too much like *Horizon*.'

'Thought you might – h'm (choke) – say that. Choose your own.'

'What do you mean?'

'Title. Years go by, one changes, wants something permanent, leave a mark. Important to have a magazine now, don't you agree, independent editor. Couldn't think of anybody more independent – h'm (choke), h'm (choke). Absolutely free hand, of course, no interference.'

'You're inviting me to edit a new magazine?' I asked incredulously. I found it hard to believe that he was serious, but H'mchoke produced from his pocket details of costings, possible distribution arrangements, projected sales figures, calculated over one, two and five years. Would the magazine rely on Arts Council backing? No, it would be an absolutely personal H'mchoke enterprise. The editor's salary was mentioned, and the sum was handsome for the year when we were talking, 1960. I said, again with uncomfortable directness, that I should want an agreement drawn up which would not permit H'mchoke to call the whole thing off after a period of a few months. H'mchoke looked injured, but said he would have no objection.

There must be a snag, but what was it? Then the snag entered the restaurant. 'I think you know Eva?' H'mchoke said. He got up and embraced her warmly.

Eva was now in her late forties, and what used to be called a fine figure of a woman. Her crowning glory was streaked with grey, but this seemed only to make its red more pronouncedly brilliant. Her manner had become distinctly gracious, and she submitted to my kiss on the cheek with a dowager's dignity. She sat down, we drank nut coffee, and H'mchoke explained that she would be the managing editor. For the most part she would be engaged with the business side of the magazine, but her knowledge of languages and her acquaintance, even friendship, with many celebrated writers in Europe and America must be helpful in giving the magazine international standing. Was my ignorance in those fields being glanced at? Very likely, although H'mchoke stressed again that all artistic and creative responsibilities (his words) would be entirely mine, and there would be no interference.

Eva sat upright while this and more was being said, rather nervously, by H'mchoke. I stayed mostly silent, pondering. No doubt Eva had set up the whole arrangement. The days of her ignorance about literary editors and reviewing practices were long past, and she was quite intelligent enough, and intellectually aware enough, to know that chatty pieces about Truman Capote's home and habits had not given her the position of *somebody* to which she had aspired in adolescence. It was authority she longed for, a position in which she would be not the interviewer but the interviewed. 'Eva

Varadi, influential managing editor of *Tempo*, said that the trend of recent British imaginative writing was away from the kitchen sink, in the direction of . . .' – that was the kind of thing. She knew also of my desire to have my own magazine. The trap had been shrewdly baited.

Another thought, not irrelevant, occurred to me. How long would her name be Varadi? H'mchoke's looks and occasional splutters were unmistakably adoring. If she had replaced Esther, Bella, Adelaide and the other recent girls, I knew Eva well enough to know that she would settle for nothing less than marriage. She would tidy up H'mchoke's domestic life, and perhaps that would be all to the good, but how much freedom would the editor have when the managing editor (ominously powerful term) was the proprietor's wife?

I said I would think about it, went home, and on the following date wrote politely saying No. A couple of days later Eva telephoned. Why had I said no? I had always wanted my own magazine, we both knew it. Was it simply that I didn't want to work with her?

'Eva', I said. 'You know it just wouldn't do.'

'Well', she said. 'All right. If that's the way you feel. I think you're wrong, but still. I can get somebody else.'

'Dozens of people.'

'Anyway. He needs someone to manage his life, run it properly. We're getting married next month. You'll get an invitation to the reception. Your wife too, of course.'

The invitation came, gilt lettering on thick card. The reception was to be held at the Savoy. Then, three days before the event, came another card saying that the wedding would not now take place, and that the reception was cancelled. I heard from another invited guest, H'mchoke's nearest approach to a close friend, what had happened. As the wedding day drew near H'mchoke, previously unmarried, had become more and more uneasy at the prospect of Eva tidying up his life as she had already tidied his apartment. No editor had been found for the magazine, and he was assailed by characteristic H'mchoke doubts about the whole project. Perhaps it would be a flop from the start and cost him tens of thousands, perhaps nobody would work with Eva, perhaps she would get all the wrong contributors and offend everybody. In the end H'mchoke cut and ran, taking off for Johannesburg in the company of a grubby little stage designer named Elspeth, and leaving a note saying it had all been a mistake.

It must have been the deepest humiliation of Eva's life. For H'mchoke the event was so traumatic that it kept him out of England for three years. Before his return Eva had made her last, and as it improbably proved successful, bid for a kind of fame.

News of it came from Alan Ross who knew that Eva and I had, as it might be said with some exaggeration, grown up together. He had been amused by the change of name, and always called her Ella. 'Did you know that your friend Ella is marrying Gilbert Threadfall?' he asked one day.

I echoed the name with astonishment. 'But he must be eighty. And he's queer.'

'Positive advantages as far as she's concerned, or so I hear. Never was very keen on a bit of the other, Ella, put off by early experiences with Symons I expect. He's not a bad painter. Neglected now, but he'll come back.'

'He'd have to arrive first.'

Nobody had ever said that Threadfall was a painter of genius, and Alan's verdict was characteristically kind. Gilbert Threadfall had painted in a great many styles, all of them derivative. In the Thirties, when surrealism arrived in Britain, Threadfall had painted a lot of pictures showing tiny Tanguy-like figures in Chirico-inspired arcades. Later he had tried Minton lushness, Nicholsonian abstracts, blank-eyed girls leaning against bits of statuary after Delvaux, melancholy near-realism imitating Balthus – there was no end to Threadfall's styles. There was a Threadfall on Alan's wall, evidently marking his discovery of Baron Ensor. It showed two clowns, one masked, the other with the mask removed to reveal a grinning death's head. They were surrounded by bits of bodies, and one clown was doing a juggling act with dismembered legs and arms.

At least, I reflected, Eva was marrying money. Threadfall had inherited a fortune from the family brewing business, and was said to have paid galleries to put on his early exhibitions. He spent the winters at a villa in the south of France, had a flat in London and a small manor house in Sussex. And although critical reception of his work had been generally cool, Threadfall had been everywhere, known everybody, at least among British painters, writers and musicians. Over the years, inevitably, he had gathered a reputation. There were Threadfalls in several provincial galleries, even one in the Tate.

'The poor old sod's on his last legs', Alan said. 'Let's hope Ella will give him a bit of comfort.'

The wedding picture I saw in a paper showed Threadfall, tall, emaciated, and looking distinctly sour, propped by a stick on one side and a smiling Eva on the other. He looked not so much on his last legs as on no legs at all, and certainly much in need of comfort. If Eva gave it to him it was not for long. Three months after the wedding he was dead.

It was a few months later that a Sunday paper began to serialise 'The Diaries of Gilbert Threadfall', edited by his widow. 'In this ruthless, no holds barred examination of the art world of his time, a famous painter dissects the work, lives and loves of his contemporaries with the skill of a master surgeon', the paper said. Threadfall had been keeping the diaries for half a century. They contained detailed descriptions of homosexual encounters involving Threadfall and many known writers and painters, savage attacks on critics who were said to have been bribed in one way or another by more successful artists, an account of a sex scandal involving a famous administrator of the arts and three underage girls hushed up only with the help of Threadfall money, the story of a girl who had killed herself when robbed of her money and deserted by a well-known poet. And all that was only the first instalment.

The diaries were written with malicious wit, and an acute

awareness of human weakness including the diarist's own. Threadfall showed himself often as fawning on people he thought had power or influence, lending them money or doing things for them in hope of favours never given. Naturally enough, the diaries gave great offence. The widow of the famous administrator protested against the slur on a dead man's name without denying the accuracy of the story, and inevitably the question was raised: should such material have been published, even if it was true? Eva was interviewed, and said she regarded it as a duty to publish diaries that remarkably reflected the period, and were in themselves works of art. 'My husband was a great painter victimised by the bureaucrats who ruled the world of art in his lifetime. It is right that the petty meanness and degraded character of many who called themselves Gilbert's friends, and accepted his help, should be made known.' At the same time, Eva revealed, she had suppressed many things in the diaries that might be thought unnecessarily wounding. That, however, was a decision which might be reconsidered, and perhaps the full diaries could be published in a year or two. There were also letters and other papers, as yet not fully examined . . .

The effect of the diaries' publication was remarkable. The prices of Threadfall paintings rose sharply, and Americans became aware of him for the first time. Profiles of Eva appeared in the tabloids, under such headings as 'The Woman Who Frightened the Art World' and 'Valiant Widow Defends "My Genius Husband"'. John Mortimer interviewed her in the *Sunday Times*, extolled her still magnificent hair, and remarked on the extreme shrewdness of her blue eyes. She told him she was beset by would-be biographers of her late husband, but had not yet made a choice among them. She would, of course, expect any biographer to consult her as to what might or might not be published. She might even, she hinted, write the book herself.

But that did not happen. Not long after publication of the diaries the D'Offay Gallery put on a retrospective show of Gilbert Threadfall's work. At the private view Eva collapsed while talking to an art critic, and was dead before the ambulance arrived. The post mortem showed a heart condition caused by a faulty valve, previously undiagnosed. The estate passed to a distant relative, who is understood to dislike publicity and to have destroyed all possibly controversial papers. In the end, however, Eva had fulfilled Ella's ambitions, however briefly. For a short time she was somebody, not an ordinary person. She had the fifteen minutes of fame Andy Warhol says is allotted to us all.

# Rupert Loxley

'EVERYBODY HAS LIVED in Oakley Street.' Rupert Loxley said this to me soon after the War ended, perhaps in 1946. The statement was evidently not literally accurate, its meaning metaphorical. Oakley Street, rather more than a quarter of a mile long, runs from the King's Road to Chelsea Embankment. Before the War, and for a few years after it, most of the houses were divided into small flats and sets of rooms, with a rapidly shifting population belonging to London's always rather vague artistic bohemia. Rupert was saying – metaphorically, metaphorically – that no matter how boringly conventional poets, novelists, artists, actors, sculptors, architects, playwrights, film directors, and writers might have become, there was a time when they had been otherwise, had succumbed to the slapdash charm of Oakley Street.

The charm, if acknowledged, belongs to the past. Nowadays Oakley Street is very different, inhabited by upwardly mobile young men in designer jeans and open-neck shirts, and their live-in partners who have jobs in 'the media'. Rupert had an apartment there only for a couple of years in the Thirties, but emotionally he stayed in Oakley Street all his life.

He was born in 1909, and at Cambridge was one of the group gathered round Jacob Bronowski and William Empson, and associated with the magazine *Experiment*. Bronowski, who later became a spell-binding performer on TV, used words like *form* and *discipline* a great deal in his youth, and Empson's permanent preoccupation with references and meanings was evident even in his conversation. Both were sometimes to be

53

met in Rupert's attic rooms. They were open and genial, even though I felt the angel Leavis brushing me with his wing when Bronowski said things like 'our generation must invent its own new notions of what is valuable, and the new notions will involve new disciplines formed by the academy, although not part of it'. In the Thirties Bronowski both wrote and talked like that.

I remember parties there, of not more than a dozen people, where talk flowed more freely than drink, and although Rupert's conversation seemed to consist largely of what might have been quotations from Bronowski and Empson, it would have been wrong to think of him as anybody's disciple. On the contrary he was a distinct and formidable personality. A large frog-like face, in colour already more puce than ruddy, was surmounted by a flattish thatch of brown hair. Exophthalmic blue eyes added to the air of froggery, but the total effect was menacing rather than absurd. His squat burly body seemed always about to burst out of his clothes. The buttons on the flowered waistcoats looked likely to give way, the jackets were always tight on the shoulders, and when he removed the jacket flesh could be seen straining to burst the seams of his shirt. At the end of long arms were thick powerful hands that often bunched into fists, and looked ready to give any trouble-maker the old one-two. Nor was this impression deceptive. Rupert had boxed at Cambridge and was said to have been the University middleweight champion, although no trophy was visible, and Rupert was not the kind of man to conceal such proof of superior merit.

Rupert, then, was far from a nullity, yet there was something about the impression he made then that was both mysterious and – I will explain the word in a moment – incomplete. The mystery related to his origins. One or two of those who had known him at Cambridge said his father was a bookmaker, others that his mother was a tart. The tart theory seemed to have no firmer basis than Rupert having been visited once or twice by women whose speech and dress were unusual and (in Cambridge terms) vulgar.

The bookmaker story was more circumstantial, portending to involve Rupert and a course bookmaker at Newbury to whom he had said 'Goodbye dad' after accepting money. But the money may have been winnings, the bookmaker's name could have been Dan, or it might have been a case of mistaken identity. Rupert himself never spoke of his family, and had no visible relatives of any kind.

And then the incompleteness – there must be another and better word, but I can't find it. He gave the impression always of waiting for something important to happen, something that would change the whole shape of his life. There seemed a vacancy behind the aggressive assurance with which he said things like 'I won't hear a word against Bill Empson', or 'Anybody who thinks Huxley wrote well is a fool'. He might shout 'Shut up, don't be such a boring bastard' if you questioned the criticism of Empson, the poetry of Eliot, the idea that a good novel could be written that was not in debt to Joyce, yet I never felt he spoke from conviction. There would always be a hint of doubt in his condemnation, as if he was saying what he knew it right to believe rather than what he believed himself. I even evolved a fantasy in which Rupert had a Daphne du Maurier romance concealed between the covers of *Ulysses*. However, he had certainly read the books he talked about. In the early Thirties Kafka had been translated by the Muirs, and Rupert was properly enthusiastic about *The Castle* and *The Great Wall of China*, yet there was a tentativeness about what he said not in tune with the physical behaviour of the frog-faced middleweight who would give you an unexpected and quite hard punch to emphasise a point.

Perhaps sex was a problem? But that seemed not to be the case, for a number of girls were to be found cooking bits of food in the Oakley Street kitchenette, most of them small, dark and European, French, Belgian or Italian. Rupert hardly seemed to know they were there, taking the cheese straws or tiny vol-au-vents offered by the current girl, and continuing to talk about the meaning of meaning or the relationship between science and poetry as if he were guest, not host.

55

It may sound as if there was nothing 'wrong' at all, as if Rupert was obviously a hanger-on, one more louse on the locks of literature, but the impression he made was not at all like that. He seemed full of anger. If the anger could be released, one felt, something interesting and perhaps important would emerge, an epic poem perhaps, or a novel longer than *Ulysses*.

Then, unexpectedly, Rupert went to Hollywood. He gave a farewell party in Oakley Street, and the ambience was rather distinctly different from that of the past. Leavisites (although that term was not then in common use) were noticeably absent, replaced by a mixture of surrealist painters – this was very early in 1936 when English artists were becoming aware of surrealism – and by loudly talkative young men discussing things like tonal montage. There were more people and much more drink than usual. A buffet was presided over by a waiter, with another waiter in charge of bottles. The current small dark woman proved to be not European but American, and to be named Lois.

'Hi,' she said to me. 'Isn't this just one hell of a party?' Uncertain whether this implied approval, I said there was more drink than usual. 'I know, I'm paying for it.' She modified this statement. 'I'm the European scout for New World Films, we're taking Rupe out to the West Coast. You know that man's a genius, he's got more ideas than a cat's got fleas. I'm not sure I always get his meaning, but my word that man's got a brain. And can he talk? I can tell you we're all excited about having him out there. Rupe's a genius, don't you agree?'

I managed to drift away without answering the question. A little later I joined a circle of admirers around Rupert, who was saying in his deep baying voice that film was the art of the future.

'People talk about cinema being killed by talking, but it just isn't so. It means the writer's come into his own, words put down on paper are going to be the basis of the art of film. You remember somebody said when he first saw a photograph, "From today painting is dead". Well, from the day people began to talk on screen the novel was dead. The Americans know it, Faulkner's out in Hollywood, so is Huxley, so's Hemingway. That's where the future of the novel is, out there.'

I had drunk enough to argue about this, to point out that after all painting wasn't dead, that I'd heard Rupert say often enough that Huxley wasn't a serious novelist, and the rumour was Faulkner hadn't got along too well in Hollywood. And what about seriousness and discipline and the meaning of meaning . . . ?

Rupert did not hear me out. 'You're a boring bastard, Julian,' he said.

I should like to be able to say that I had made some adequately insulting reply, but all I managed was something on the lines of 'Fuck you, Rupert,' before leaving the party.

In Hollywood I afterwards heard, I think from Anthony Powell who was there at much the same time, Rupert suffered the not uncommon fate of being left idle for several weeks. He was then put to writing scripts for Westerns, and later did some dialogue for a film about Philo Vance, I suppose on the basis that a highly sophisticated Englishman was just the person to write dialogue about a super-sophisticated American detective. Nothing he wrote was used, and after a few months whatever agreement he had expired, and was not renewed.

It must have been more than a year later that I met Rupert in the Plough, the pub just off Chancery Lane used by contributors to the *New Outlook*. The weekly was at this time firmly political, with only three or four pages at the back end given to literature. In the past Rupert had shown no interest in politics, so that it was a surprise to find him in earnest conversation with the paper's expert on East European affairs, a Polish ex-Communist who called herself Elsie Smith, her own name being a jumble of consonants hopelessly jarring to an English eye. Elsie's nose had been broken in some street fighting and badly reset, her teeth had been knocked out when she was caught running an underground press in Poland and Colonel Beck's police put her in prison. She gave the impression of having put on the first clothes she happened to come across. Yet Elsie still, in her forties, looked extremely attractive to somebody almost twenty years her junior. In spite or because of what she had been through – imprisonment in three countries when helping to edit forbidden magazines, expulsion from the Party because she expressed doubts about Stalin's agricultural policy, subsequent betrayal to the Polish police – she remained unquenchably optimistic about the eventual triumph of a socialism both virtuous and tolerant. The virtue and the tolerance, words which will look odd and even absurd to the political young today, were tenets taken for granted by many socialists then, Elsie and myself included, with the difference that her belief had been practically tested. For Elsie her betrayal, the internecine war within the Polish Communist Party, the self-perpetuating bureaucracy of other European parties including the French and German – these were mere aberrations that would be wiped out, cancelled, when socialism gained power throughout Europe. To that conundrum posed by the youthful Christopher Isherwood: do you support nice friendly people whose ideas are wrong, or unpleasant people whose ideas are right? Elsie would have given an unhesitating verdict in favour of the latter. If such an answer seems incredible or unintelligible today, so much the worse (Elsie would have said and so would I) for today.

This will make it clear why I was surprised to see Elsie in the saloon bar with Rupert, pint glasses in front of them, she talking with her usual exuberant eagerness, Rupert listening with apparent absorption. Surprised too that he greeted me with a bear's hug, expressed his delight at seeing me. His face was a shade redder than it had been in Oakley Street days, his waistcoat no less extravagant.

What did Rupert want with Elsie, what interest could Elsie conceivably have in Rupert? The *New Outlook* was publishing a series of pamphlets on such subjects as nationalization of the railways, the need for a Socialist Popular Front throughout

Europe, the links between arms dealers and big business, and as their conversation continued I gathered that Rupert was going to write one of these. The title escapes me, but the subject was the clash between liberal writers and directors and studio bosses in Hollywood, and the struggle to create the Screen Writers' Guild. Elsie was enthusiastic, believing apparently that the pamphlet would have the effect of uniting screen writers and directors on both sides of the Atlantic in support of the Republican cause in Spain. I thought but did not say that Rupert's time in Hollywood provided a slender base for writing such a pamphlet. Then Elsie, with a kiss and a 'Bless you, my darlings', was gone. I asked Rupert what he'd made of Hollywood.

'Disgusting. Words can't describe it. Philistines leading the Gadarene swine over the cliff.' What about the art of film, I asked maliciously, the film as today's replacement of the novel? Rupert snorted.

'All that is perfectly true. How many people read a novel? Generally a few hundred, where millions see a film. But all Hollywood does is turn out pap for the masses.'

'Those are the films the millions want to see, however, isn't that so?'

'In America they've been taught and bribed to like it, that's the nature of capitalist society. And they export their filth here, contaminate us with it. Eisenstein couldn't work in America, you know why? Because there can't be any art without social responsibility, and there's no social responsibility in Hollywood. Except among the screen writers,' he added as an afterthought.

A few minutes later we were joined by Norris Tibbs, who was as strong a socialist as Elsie, but viewed the future with a pessimism that was the obverse of Elsie's determined optimism. Both had their eyes set on eventual triumph, but where Elsie expected it to usher in an artistic renaissance, Norris thought nothing but the crudest propaganda art could be produced in a socialist society. Now, with a look of distaste, he handed me two novels by English proletarian writers.

'These are crap, but I suppose we have to do them. Six hundred words in two weeks, all right?'

Rupert picked up one of them. 'Jack Maguire's in Spain.'

Norris turned from ordering his beer. 'I daresay.'

'It's not *daresay*.' Rupert's voice rose, his colour deepened alarmingly. 'Jack's out there, he's fighting for the Spanish Republic, you can't use words like crap about what he writes.' Norris made no reply, but hunched his narrow shoulders, half turned away, and began to talk to the pretty barmaid. Rupert transferred his attention to me. He picked up the other book, rifled through the pages. 'These are serious books about real people, right? Brushing them aside, that's just what those bastards do in Hollywood, and what happens? The public gets fed nothing but candyfloss. Hallo, darling.'

'Hi,' said the small dark woman by his side. Rupert introduced her as his wife, she said we'd met. It was Lois. A few minutes later they left, to attend a fund-raising rally aimed at buying arms for the Spanish Republic. Lois was on the committee. She was both proprietorial with Rupert and evidently proud of him, her genius safely corralled. When they had gone Norris sighed.

'It *is* crap, you know,' he said, referring to the Jack Maguire novel. 'Why are all the books on the right side so bad?' It was not a question to which he expected an answer. 'The best writers are all social villains, that's a law.'

'Tibbs's law?' He nodded. 'But only British law, it doesn't apply elsewhere.'

'Agreed,' he said gloomily. 'He's talented, you know, Loxley, immensely intelligent. But no good. It's the national disease.'

'I'd no idea he was married.'

'You know why? Lois's family owns a few small oil wells. Rupert says he married her to preserve his art, but where's the art? It just means he's living high on the hog.'

'Elsie's asked him to do one of the *Outlook* pamphlets. About Hollywood.'

'He'll never write it.'

Norris, as often, was correct, and right too about Rupert living high on the hog. He and Lois had a house in Tite Street which became a centre for all sorts of progressive activities. There were piano recitals, poetry readings, an exhibition of pictures, most of them in the service of raising funds for Spain. And there were parties, designed to promote a Popular Front that would embrace all anti-Fascist people and movements from the Labour Party to the Peace Pledge Union. Labour politicians and intellectuals were to be seen at these parties, Stafford Cripps, Nye Bevan, Harold Laski, along with volunteers back from Spain and a sprinkling of anti-Chamberlain Conservatives like Harold Macmillan and Winston Churchill. It was said that Churchill had been seen deep in conversation with Victor Gollancz and the Communist Party secretary Harry Pollitt. Rupert and Lois also went to dinners at the House of Commons and at the American Embassy, which numbered several Popular Front sympathizers among the junior staff. I write about this from hearsay, for I was both too unimportant and too heretical about the Popular Front to have been on the invitation list.

In retrospect I suppose this period might be called the apogee of Rupert's career, although it did not look like that at the time. I saw him rarely, once at an auction of paintings, the proceeds going (of course) to the Spanish Republic. He was wearing one of his most splendid waistcoats, purple and grey edged with gold braid, his face almost matching the waistcoat's purple. He greeted me genially but with a certain loftiness, which showed when I said it was an impressive collection of paintings.

'I didn't need to twist any arms, just a word was enough. Ben and Henry were naturally sympathetic, and as soon as Picasso knew where the money was going he sent over that little drawing.'

'Ben and Henry equals Nicholson and Moore? I didn't know they were friends of yours.'

'If you're around in London you can't avoid meeting people. It's inevitable.'

'Where's Lois?'

'She's around somewhere, I expect.' He glared at me, the pale blue eyes looked as if they might burst from their sockets. 'We're independent, you know, we only make the beast with two backs at night. I don't control her nor she me, you understand?' He gripped my shoulders. It seemed to me that as in the past rage was pent up in him, the 'agony of flame that cannot singe a sleeve' Yeats wrote about. Then he let go and said in a more reasonable tone, 'As a matter of fact I've been very busy lately, I'm working on a biography of William Morris. Jonathan suggested it and I felt I couldn't say no, but it means burning a lot of midnight oil.'

One of the superfluity of girls hanging about handing out programmes and answering questions – they all looked like fashion models – plucked at his arm, and he left me without explaining the identity of Jonathan. What surname could he have, however, but Cape?

That must have been one of the last such shows or parties. A few weeks later Madrid surrendered, Franco's victory was complete, and Rupert and Lois parted company. I heard the news from Elsie, who expressed concern.

'What will he do now? He has nothing, you understand, no money and nowhere to live. That bitch has left him flat.'

'So where is he living?'

'In my flat.' Elsie gave the grin that was attractive even though it showed her false teeth. 'Somebody has to look after him.'

'Did he ever write the pamphlet about Hollywood?'

'He began it, but there's no point in it now. We'll have war in Europe in twelve months.'

'He's supposed to be writing a biography of William Morris, he must have had an advance.'

'Rupert has to be looked after, he has been hurt. You think I'm an old bag out cradle-snatching, all right, my darling, you think what you like but I tell you there is something special about Rupert. One day he will surprise us all.'

It was through Elsie that when the war came, in a few weeks rather than the twelve months she had predicted, Rupert got a job in the BBC. She knew, or so it sometimes seemed to me, every dissident, whether Marxist, socialist or anarchist, who had come to Britain from central Europe, and she helped several of them to get jobs in the BBC's foreign sections. Through one of these, a woman named Miriam something or other, she got Rupert into the French section. Within a few weeks he had gone to live with this Miriam. I asked Elsie how she felt about it, and she shrugged.

'No use having feelings, feelings are no use any more. Things happen, whether you like them or not they happen, you have to accept them. Nothing else you can do.'

'No feelings involved, that's all there is to it?'

'There's never anything else to it, the rest is just imagination.' She grinned. 'In the future, under socialism, perhaps there may be something else, but now there isn't.'

I saw Rupert once or twice in the Café Royal with Miriam, a tall thin dark woman instead of his usual small dark ones. She kept a guardian eye on Rupert, as if he was a valuable animal who must be given a certain amount of freedom but not allowed to escape. The occasional uneasy turning of his big head and thick neck encouraged this impression of confinement. One evening he said suddenly, 'I volunteered, you know, the week the war broke out. Wouldn't have me.'

When I asked why not he said vaguely that he was all churned up inside, and indeed something within him did seem to be moving about, causing pain or irritation. Was perhaps an inner churning responsible for his constant sweating, mottled face and purplish lips?

'Like Dylan,' he added. I said I understood Dylan Thomas was a conscientious objector, and he glared at me. 'I won't hear a word against Dylan. Only two great poets in our generation, Wystan and Dylan, won't hear anything against them.' We became involved in a long argument, of a kind fairly common in the early months of the War, about conscientious objection, opposition to Fascism, the merits and defects of

63

Hitler and Stalin, a pointless squabble from which Miriam took him away.

After my call-up, early in 1942, I saw and heard nothing of Rupert. A little less than two years later I was invalided out of the Army, got a job off the Strand, and found he and I were using the same Finch's pub. He was still apparently in the French section of the BBC at Bush House, although he was vague about what he did, and vaguer still when I asked about Miriam. Who did I mean, what was her other name? I could not remember her surname, but described her.

'*Her*,' Rupert said contemptuously. 'I don't know what happened to *her*. I have no connection with *her*.' His pop eyes glared. He had never been a good-tempered man, but was now liable to become enraged by any views opposed to his own, and to express the disapproval by violence. Whatever had been churning inside him was, it might now be said, boiling over. He was barred from Finch's after an assault on a weedy BBC radio producer who insisted that Sidney Keyes was a better poet than Dylan Thomas, and we met thereafter in the George at the top of Fleet Street, and occasionally in a pub at the back of the Law Courts.

'We' means a random and changing collection of BBC people, Fleet Street journalists, and a few odds and ends like me. George Orwell, then literary editor of *Tribune*, was one of them, and Orwell on one occasion took exception to a remark of Rupert's about being in favour of everything first-class like Catholicism and Zionism, and opposed to such second-rate faiths and ideas as Methodism, liberalism and Parliamentary democracy. All that was nonsense, Orwell said, Catholicism was the most reactionary of religions, Zionism's success would wreck any prospect of a socialist Jewish state. The argument rumbled round like thunder until closing time. I remember Norman Cameron making a spirited defence of Catholicism, and somebody else – Tosco Fyvel perhaps – saying Zionism was the only hope for Jewry. Afterwards Orwell said Rupert was a dangerous man.

'If the Germans came here you could make a list of

those who'd oppose them and those who'd collaborate. Loxley would be one of the collaborators.' When I said Rupert had actively supported the Spanish Republic Orwell shook his narrow head. 'He doesn't have any opinions of his own, just wants to be in fashion. If the Germans were in power and the right sort of people were going to the parties they gave, your friend Loxley would be there too. He'd call it accepting reality, something like that.'

I thought and still think that was unjust, but there was no doubt of Rupert's anxiety to be seen at the right parties and to say intellectually fashionable things. Not long after the War ended he proclaimed himself an Existentialist. When I asked what he meant I received one of his glares.

'What I mean is there's no fucking hope any more in mass movements, none at all. Never was, I daresay. The only real thing now is the idea of the person, the truth of individual feelings. Have you read Sartre on morality? Or Camus? Well, you should. Have you seen *Huis Clos*? "Hell is other people", my god that's true.'

This conversation took place in a dingy apartment in Camden Town, two rooms and a kitchenette, where he was living with a young actress named Zoe Zukins (at least, she called herself that) who doted on him. Rupert had lost his BBC job after some great row that had ended in his partly demolishing an office. Zoe, who had rich parents, paid the rent of the flat. She was not by nature tidy or cleanly, and sometimes Rupert's waistcoats would be dirty, and both he and Zoe would smell rather high. He was said to spend a lot of time in the Mandrake Club with drunken artists like Gerald Wilde, but still came to the George, although he was now so quarrelsome that people tended to avoid him and eventually he was barred from the pub. Then I read a paragraph in one of the popular dailies which said that young actress Zoe Zukins had jumped to her death beneath an Underground train at Leicester Square. A picture of Zoe gave her a film starlet's glamour that she had not possessed in life.

I sent Rupert a note of condolence to which he made no reply, but didn't see him for months. News filtered through, of course, some of it contradictory. Zoe had been drunk and, always slightly inclined to vertigo, pitched in front of the train. There had been a frightful quarrel, Rupert had hit her, she'd left the flat swearing that she would kill herself; and so on. The stories about Rupert said he had been broken up by her death, had given up flowered waistcoats and now dressed entirely in black except for a white shirt, had gone to live with Elsie who turned him out because he was drunk every night. When I saw Elsie she said he had stayed with her for a time.

'And you turned him out?'

'Don't believe all you hear.' She tapped my arm. 'There is something in Rupert, more than there is in you or me or most people. You are not to joke about him.' When I said I hadn't been joking she shook her head. 'Oh yes you had, you and everybody else. The English joke about everything, it is their curse. But you will see. Or perhaps you won't see, but still what I say is true.'

'I feel sorry for Zoe.'

'Why, yes. Of course. But Zoe was a nut.' She gave the grin that showed her false teeth. 'That is all there is to be said about Zoe.'

'And what should one say about Rupert?'

'He is an original. He is not a carbon copy.'

My next, almost my last, meeting with Rupert was in the Savoy Grill, to which I had been taken by my then publisher Victor Gollancz. In some matters a mean man, Victor could also be ostentatiously hospitable. Lunch was offered rarely to a minor author like me, but it was at the Savoy Grill rather than some less conspicuous establishment. Across the room Rupert was lunching with one of those women who look neither young nor middle-aged nor even old, but present to the world a mask of such enamelled stylish beauty that one would be reluctant even to ask whether it corresponded at all with physical reality. To my surprise Victor waved to her enthusiastically. He was pleased by my ignorance.

'Mary Lou Hoffman, owns . . .' And he mentioned a fashion magazine that prided itself on offering an up-to-date view of the arts. 'Amazing woman, sixty-five, might be thirty-five, demon for work, says it's because she's vegetarian, teetotaller, non-smoker. I envy her.' We were at the coffee stage, and he lighted one of his big cigars. 'Comes over from New York every couple of years to shake up the paper, they all tremble with terror until she's gone back. Don't know what she wants with young Loxley.' It was Victor's amiable habit to refer to almost everybody as young. He once called somebody a boy, then corrected himself. 'I suppose I should say young man, he's forty-two.' I asked how he knew Rupert. He waved his cigar. 'Doing a big book for us about William Morris, very exciting. Great man, Morris.'

Mary Lou Hoffman stopped at our table. Her enormous false eyelashes fluttered like butterfly wings. 'Lovely to *see* you, Victor, and looking so *well*.' Rupert stood beside her, not glowering but almost demure, waistcoat gleaming, hair parted in the middle, bulk confined as if by a corset. 'I want you to meet our new literary editor, Rupert Loxley.'

Victor said heartily that she could not have made a better choice, mentioned William Morris, offered celebratory brandy. Rupert refused. Mary Lou raised a much-jewelled hand, placed it on his shoulder.

'You are not to lead Rupert into bad ways. He doesn't smoke, and he never drinks more than one glass of wine a day. I am sick and tired of *my* people in *my* offices contaminating *my* desks with filthy nicotine and returning from *long* drunken luncheons and pretending to work while simply *fuddled*.' She looked challengingly at Victor and at me. 'One of the things I liked about Rupert was his honesty, he *admitted* taking a glass of wine every day.' Her Cupid's-bow mouth cracked in a smile. 'Mind you, that's a habit we'll hope to change.'

It would be nice to say that Rupert winked at me, but he did not. I looked down at the tablecloth.

Rupert lasted four months at the magazine. Then he

passed out in the office one evening, woke at nine o'clock, broke down the door of the flat the editor kept for occasions when it was inconvenient to go home, and was found asleep there in the morning. A telex from Mary Lou in New York confirmed his instant dismissal.

Not very long after this I went into the Jermyn Street Turkish baths, now no more, and in one of the steam rooms saw a towel-wrapped Rupert, the visible parts of him bright red, huddled in a corner. He seemed neither pleased nor annoyed to see me, and hardly spoke until I said Angus Wilson and Kingsley Amis seemed to mark something new in English fiction. At that he sat up, the partly-dropped towel revealing a mass of quivering mottled flesh.

'What was it for, will you tell me that, what was it all for?' He saw my look of incomprehension. 'Books I mean, painting, music, everything. Joyce and Max Ernst and de Chirico and the twelve-tone scale, Duchamps and his ready-mades. We already had Dickens and Trollope, Galsworthy and Bennett and Wells, why not stop there, eh, you tell me? What do we want with Wilson and Amis, are they telling us anything?'

'Have you read them?'

'Don't need to, read enough, too much. No more writing, no more pictures, they're all over. What I mean is, if you've got Munnings – no, fuck it, don't mean Munnings, say John. There was John and Sickert and Cézanne and Matisse, what the fuck did we want with de Chirico? Or Tanguy? Or Dali? Or Joyce and all that?' He put out big hands and shook me. The towel dropped completely, showing small penis, bulging thighs. 'I've spent my life trying to understand it all, and what was the point? Can you tell me?'

Speech has its banalities, but so has silence. I adhered to the banalities of silence. Rupert looked at me yearningly with popping bloodshot eyes. 'Once things were possible, isn't that so? Remember Oakley Street and Bill Empson? Doesn't write anything now, no poems. Great man, wise man, Bill Empson. He knows if you're any good writing can't be done now, everything first-rate is over. Ever read Djuna Barnes?'

I said I had read Djuna Barnes. 'She wrote well. Once I thought I—' He did not complete the sentence. '"There is a point beyond which there is no turning back. This is the point that must be reached." Know who wrote that?'

'Kafka.'

'Kafka, yes.' He gathered the towel round him. 'Let's get out of this place, have a drink.'

He died a few weeks later of a heart attack, in Shepherds Bush. Loises and Miriams and Zoes had abandoned him, and he was living alone in a bed-sitting room. The refrigerator was filled with food, and half of a large chocolate cream cake was on a table near him. His body was not found for a week.

# Charlie and Liz Paradon

I REMEMBER PEOPLE for the most part by single characteristics, a particular wave of the hand, a shuffling of feet, a nose set to one side, a shy or charming smile. With Charlie Paradon, however, it was a phrase, or a collection of phrases likely to follow one another in quick succession. 'You just can't *say* that kind of thing, you can't *use* arguments like that, it's not possible to *make* that assumption.'

Writing those words on the page I see Charlie's face, round and ruddy and topped by crisp curly black hair, eager and innocent brown eyes hiding behind horn-rimmed spectacles almost permanently in need of minor repairs. The subjects about which the phrases were used might be the activities of Communists in the trade unions, the benefits and drawbacks of nationalisation, attacks by Jews on British forces in Palestine and the blowing up of the King David Hotel. The time was the late Forties, when such matters were current topics of discussion, and Charlie argued about them at length and quite unsubdually. He always sounded reasonable, and began by appearing to admit his opponent's case, which he would then turn at a right angle, or even on its head. '*Of course* the Commies are out to increase Party influence inside the unions, the thing is you find they're always the hardest workers, they use the Labour Party and the Party uses them . . . maybe nationalisation doesn't make the mines produce more coal, that's not the point, the point of nationalisation is more pay and better conditions for workers . . . you can't *use* arguments like saying the Jews are terrorists and just leave it at that, the Jews have been under the thumb of the

British and treated as second-class citizens for years, killing innocent people with bombs is something I hate as much as you do, but you shouldn't make the assumption all Jewish opposition to British rule comes from terrorists . . .' Charlie's little wife Liz sat on a sofa in their living room, eyes shining with admiration, nodding approval.

I first met Charlie at one of the Leftish meetings held in the Salisbury pub in St Martin's Lane, and found that he lived not far away from me in Blackheath. He was a lecturer at LSE, his speciality the economies of what were beginning to be called the Iron Curtain countries, about which he would offer a stream of figures relating to the increased production of everything from wheat to pig iron, a stream undammable because nobody listening to him could quote figures in contradiction. Liz worked in the housing department of the local council, and would tell horror stories about slum housing in the past, along with visionary tales of what was being done, and still more what would be done in the near future, to provide what she called adequate housing units for everybody.

Charlie and Liz may sound like classic bores but that wasn't so, or perhaps I should say I didn't find them so then. In the years immediately after the War many of us (an 'us' I shan't bother to define) agreed with most of the things Charlie Paradon said, even though he went on about them a bit, and the accounts by Liz of her local council work gave her almost saintly status. I suppose on the level of ideas simply, we'd all been influenced by Ayer's *Language, Truth and Logic* and the moral relativism implicitly advanced in it, so that terrorism practised by the Jews against the British seemed justifiable, and the Government's pro-Arab stance outrageous. Our feelings about Jewish terrorism had some similarity to those of blacks nowadays who say there can be no such thing as black racism in a white-run country, or homosexuals and feminists who regard mere tolerance as a form of opposition. But Charlie and Liz weren't aggressive in the way blacks, homosexuals and feminists tend to be nowadays, and their hearts were obviously in the right place. They clearly meant well.

There was something comic about Charlie Paradon, even about his name, which as Norris Tibbs said seemed to have begun as a paradox and ended up as a disinfectant. And the comic earnestness with which he spoke was mixed with an ingenuousness that gave him a sort of charm. He laid down the law with those 'You can't say that kind of thing' edicts, yet there was a probing, uncertain quality about what he said. It was as if he was using a foreign language, skilfully but not with assurance, and it came as no surprise to learn that his parents were Jews who had left Russia after the Revolution, when Charlie was four or five years old. The family name had been something like Paradolsky, and I suppose Paradon had seemed easily pronounceable, without being what would have been in Dr Paradon's case absurdly English. Absurdly, because he had never truly mastered the language, and his appearance was evidently central European, or at any rate not English.

He was a small man, with a permanently angry expression rather like that of Alf Garnett in the TV series, and so far as I know he had no right to be called Doctor. He owned a small factory on the outskirts of Birmingham that manufactured ball bearings, and Charlie had been to King Edward VI School and Birmingham University. Charlie was affectionate to his parents when they came to stay (his mother Irma was near to being an archetypal Jewish momma), but also slightly apologetic about them. They were so obviously unassimilated foreigners, and he had spent his adult life working hard at being English. They were orthodox Jews, and he had no religion. They disapproved of the habits, ideas and no doubt morals of most of Charlie's friends, and Dr Paradon was not reluctant to say so. Their disapproval didn't extend to Liz, whose antecedents were impeccably English (father a Vicar in Devon), and who had produced two children, Adam and Vicky, who were not quite teenagers in those early post-war days.

Charlie and Liz were casually hospitable, their big rambling house always full of people, exiles from Eastern Europe, students who acted as au pairs looking after the children while the parents were attending meetings, people met at conferences about the future of Europe, the nature of Titoism, the problems of post-war housing, the importance of co-ordinating transport systems, the moral problems of politics and the political difficulties of morality. There were drinks parties at which the number of people was often so large that the drink ran out rather quickly, and dinner parties at which the other guests frequently turned out to be people either Charlie or Liz had met for the first time a few days earlier at a conference. In the late Forties rationing was still strict, but Liz was an ingenious cook, and would produce mounds of rice with a good many bits of unidentifiable but unquestionable meat in them, or masses of potato patties with some unknown ingredient that gave them a distinctive flavour. The guests ate these and similar dishes enthusiastically, and would probably not have flinched from whalemeat and snoek, which were about at the time, since what they really came for was argument.

Sometimes they included people whose ideas were at odds – a Titoist Yugoslav might sit next to an ardent British Stalinist, a believer in the total elimination of all private schooling encounter an Etonian or Wykehamist who insisted that centres of educational excellence must be preserved, and so on. The difference between such arguments and superficially similar ones that go on today was that at the Paradons we were all really on the same side, with even the Wykehamists agreeing that private education must slowly be phased out, and the pro- and anti-Titoists never for a moment considering the possibility of a return to Parliamentary rule in Yugoslavia. Nowadays advocates of state control in any sphere of life whisper their heresies. In those days, and not only at the Paradons, the desirable nature of state control was unquestioned, the arguments only about how it could best be achieved. I remember one evening, after a man from the

Rumanian Embassy had spent some time calling Charlie a snivelling Kautskyist and describing Liz's activities as putting poultices on a patient suffering from gangrene, Adam asking his father why the man had been so angry. Charlie, who had remained what must have been maddeningly patient, injecting a few figures about Rumanian oil production into the tirade against him as a bourgeois economist, said when people felt strongly they sometimes said things they didn't quite mean. Adam, who looked like a pocket version of his father minus the spectacles, said perhaps it was best not to feel strongly about anything. Charlie patted him on the head.

'What you have to do is argue it out. Always argue it out.'

Adam jerked a dirty thumb after the departed Rumanian. 'But would Mr Crolez let you argue with him?'

'That's one of the problems we've got to solve, persuading people to argue things out. Perhaps we may not solve it, but you will.' Charlie put an arm round his son's shoulders, and kissed him. 'Remember, if Liz and I are too busy to listen to you sometimes, it's your future we're working for. As for us, maybe we shall never see it.'

This sounds like the most sickly guff, but Charlie and Liz were genuinely devoted to their children, though only intermittently attentive to them, and at the time I found his sentiments rather moving. Perhaps this was because that vision of a world where people of all persuasions behaved well to each other seemed more plausible then than it does now. A couple of lines of Tom Hood stick in my mind as an emblem of that possible world:

> For the lion and Adam were company,
> And the tiger him beguiled.

We should all have known better. The lions and tigers never became company for Adam, either in Hood's poem or for Charlie's son.

The end of the Forties, when he became an adviser to the Government on Eastern Europe, was Charlie Paradon's apogee. I never discovered just what he did, but the effect was to fill the Paradon home with different, politically more important people. A good many of them were Labour MPs on the Bevanite wing of the party, but there were just as many from what were beginning to be called Soviet satellites. It would no longer be just 'a man from the Rumanian Embassy' one met, but a First Secretary or even the Ambassador. The Poles were back-slappingly genial, the Bulgarians came in pairs and one seemed always to be watching the other, there was a Hungarian who spoke perfect English and often mentioned Arthur Koestler, and several Czechs conspicuous by their gold teeth. The Russians were absent but the others, MPs and East Europeans alike, listened to Charlie with flattering attentiveness as he talked about spheres of influence, the effects of the Marshall Plan, and the chances of turning round the Yugoslavs so that they relinquished Titoist heresies and were brought back into what he called the progressive camp.

There seemed to be a good deal more food and drink about now, and perhaps the rumours that the Paradons received a special Government hospitality allowance were true. It became practically impossible to argue with Charlie in this phase of his career, when his usual mass of figures would be supported by 'I happened to be talking to the Ambassador last week and he confirmed that . . .' whatever Charlie had been maintaining was correct. 'You just can't *say* that kind of thing' might now be accompanied by something like a smirk. What did Liz think of Charlie's rise to – well, not power, but certainly a position of influence? She had been made head of the housing department, and her name was in the local paper almost every week, but at home she was very much subsidiary to her husband. Only an occasional tightening of her rather thin lips suggested she might resent this, but at the evening talkfests she had often a little cluster of her own associates, mostly women Council members, with whom no doubt she planned strategies for getting her housing plans accepted. She took almost no part in Charlie's international discussions.

Charlie's celebrity – the word doesn't seem too strong, for his views were often quoted in weekly magazines – alienated his parents, after they paid a visit during which Dr Paradon had a shouting match with a Pole about the benefits of private enterprise.

'I have money but I wuk for it, I wuk for it all the days of my life', Dr Paradon cried, to which the Pole, some sort of Government official, replied that he had grown fat off the backs of his workers. Dr Paradon took this literally. 'I am not fat', he shouted. '*You* are fat, you are fat burrowcrat'. Afterwards he rebuked his son for associating with men bent on destroying society, and for neglecting the moral welfare of his children. Vicky had been caught stealing money at school, and the Paradons had responded by increasing her weekly allowance. Irma made soothing noises during these and other arguments, saying 'Not so loud, you should not be so loud' to her husband. He would reply that there was no harm in being loud when you spoke the truth, a remark that would have been more effective if he had not called it the troot. The truth remains true however the word is pronounced, yet when it becomes verbally something between toot and trout the effect is hard to take seriously. In the face of much Garnettish abuse Charlie was patient and Liz silent, but a sense of strain was inevitable, and the visits of the senior Paradons became rarer.

In this time of his celebrity Charlie did not smarten himself up in appearance. He still wore baggy trousers, a woollen tie and a scruffy-looking sports jacket, when he sat in on meetings as adviser to a Minister. His spectacles were still often kept together by sticky tape. A new phrase was added to his armoury, 'He' (less often she) 'knows what it's all about'. Nye Bevan knew what it was all about in relation to health, Ernie Bevin didn't know in relation to Palestine, Eastern Europe, or almost any other sphere of foreign policy. Stalin knew what it was all about but Churchill didn't although he had known in the War, Cripps knew what it was all about in relation to monetary policy and the need for rationing. There was a category of people who knew what it was all about, but were for various reasons on the wrong side, President Truman and Lord Beaverbrook among them. It may sound as if Charlie was simply in favour of ruthlessness (he was fond of quoting Stalin's alleged wartime question about the Pope: 'How many divisions has he got?'), but that was not true. Knowing what it was all about implied awareness of what was going to happen – in world politics, the British economy, Israel, African countries – and acting in accordance with that knowledge. It was part of the *history is on our side* belief that marked Charlie's generation. History, as Auden said, was the operator, the inexorable and dangerous ruler that neither helped nor pardoned the defeated, and when held one moment burnt the hand. Charlie was not much of a poetry reader, but he would have agreed with all those sentiments. It felt comfortable to be on history's side.

The Labour Government's defeat in the 1951 election was a great shock to him. He had inveighed against some aspects of Government policy, but that the Tories should regain power seemed to him incomprehensible. He had regarded the election in the previous year when Labour scraped home as a hiccup, and everything he said and believed in was bound up with the assumption that Labour would be in power during any foreseeable future. A couple of weeks after the election he was still shaking his head, and saying 'How could people have done it, how could they have been such fools?' Now, at a stroke or at a vote, Charlie's days of celebrity and influence were over. Of course he attended no more Ministerial conferences, and although the Paradons still gave parties, the number of Labour MPs and foreign notables to be seen at them had much diminished. Some of the parties took on the character of wakes, as laments about what might or should have been filled the air. Charlie was still called to occasional Opposition meetings as adviser on Eastern Europe, but his involvement was half-hearted, for of what interest was it to have the right policies if you lacked power to carry them out?

Liz was noticeably less affected by the election result. She had become a member of the London County Council (the Greater London Council not yet in being), and was a member of several committees. Her interest was now almost wholly in local politics, and she showed an occasional touch of impatience with the dismal tone of the discussions in which Charlie and his friends engaged. There were practical things to be done, Liz and her friends suggested, and Charlie would do well to take an interest in local government, which retained a lot of power whatever they liked to do or say in the Westminster talking shop. At the parties, where people flowed from one large untidy room to another, Liz and her group now formed a coherent unit, ignoring as much as possibly any who joined them in the hope of gossiping about Kent cricket, Charlton football, the iniquities of Toryism, or even changes in the Soviet Union after Stalin.

The attack on Suez and the Hungarian rebellion against Communist rule both came late in 1956. On the day the Russian tanks rolled into Budapest Vicky Paradon was knocked over and killed by a motorbike. She stepped out from behind a van parked near a zebra crossing, and so was not quite on the crossing herself. The bike rider said she appeared suddenly and he couldn't have avoided her, a couple of witnesses at the inquest gave evidence that he was going very fast and couldn't have stopped if she had been on the crossing instead of a couple of yards away from it, the jury's verdict was accidental death. At the time of the accident Charlie was at a meeting called by some Left-wing group or other to decide whether they should support the Russian invasion (they thought they shouldn't), Liz in Paris with a delegation looking at new housing developments. Vicky died in hospital before they could be reached. Adam, who was still at school, was with her when she died.

Since neither Charlie nor Liz had any religion, I was surprised that the funeral involved a Church service. It seemed that Vicky had insisted on being confirmed, and had said she would join Christian Aid and work overseas when she grew up (she was nearly fifteen when she died). Afterwards about thirty of us went back to the Blackheath house, where the baked meats consisted of thick-cut sandwiches, sausage rolls and cheesecake. Dr Paradon was disgusted.

'You do not know what should be done', he said. 'You have no respek. Look at you.' It was true that Charlie was wearing his usual clothes, not perfectly clean grey trousers, check woollen shirt, pullover and sports jacket. Liz wore a black dress and jet earrings, and the occasion seemed to have improved her appearance. Dr Paradon muttered on, the words *disgusting* and *faithless* audible. Irma hushed him. Charlie said it did not matter, Vicky had gone. His father, face very red, exploded.

'Gone, she is not gone. Everything lives. She would be here now, my little Vicky, if you were good father. What do you do but talk, talk, nonsense all of it, we do this, we do that, you do nothing.' He transferred his attention to Liz. 'And you, if you were true mother, at home with little Vicky, she would still be living. But you are in Paris, what do you do in Paris?'

Liz had a thin but penetrating voice. 'I was looking at new blocks of flats, models for what we shall build here to house people better. How would it have helped Vicky if I had been at home?'

Dr Paradon ignored the last sentence. 'Flats, flats, who tells you English people want to live in flats, they like their little houses.'

'They'll have to learn to like what they get, then, won't they?' The lines of Liz's mouth almost disappeared, her eyes sparkled with anger. 'I don't know why you should think you're an authority on what English people want.'

Dr Paradon, mortally wounded, placed a hand on his heart and turned away. Irma shook her head reproachfully and went with him. Adam, now taller than his father and no longer a replica of him, had been listening. He said, 'I should have thought you could get through today without quarrelling.'

79

'I was not quarrelling. It was an argument.'

Adam went across to talk to his grandparents. Charlie, usually so vocal, had been standing stock still nearby. Now he hurried from the room as if in response to an urgent message. He had not returned when I left.

Was it a public or a personal event, Vicky's death or the suppression of Hungary's attempt at independence, that changed Charlie Paradon? Whatever the cause, he seemed to have been abandoned by the certainties through which he had attained a reputation. Another victim of the god that failed? But Charlie had never adhered to the Communist Party line, nor on the other hand did he revile the Soviet Government because it had, as he put it, made a tragic mistake in Hungary. On the surface his attitudes changed very little. He argued, as he had always done, that the coming of socialism was inevitable, he was still busy with meetings designed to get the Tories out and at the same time oust the Right-wingers now in control of the Labour Party. He wrote occasional articles in the *New Statesman, Tribune* and the *New Outlook*, his classes at LSE were still well attended, students still came to Blackheath for coffee and chat. Even so, the old certainty that there was an obviously right line to be followed by anybody with intelligence had gone, and 'You just can't *say* that kind of thing' was a phrase now remote from his lips. As I look back, the Fifties seem to have been one defeat after another for Charlie's beliefs, with no cheer to be had through East European developments except perhaps in the rise of Krushchev, the Tory Governments first of Churchill, then of Eden and Macmillan winning elections, and the Labour Party swinging right with little sign that it might regain power.

These defeats were, I think, linked in his mind with Vicky's death, not so much because he loved her as that she symbolised the future. I remember an occasion two or three years before she died when some professional educationalist asked Charlie how much responsibility he and Liz felt for their children's education. Charlie was at his most oratorical.

'Total responsibility in one sense, in another none at

all. Adam and Vicky are going through the State system, because in our view it should be universal. At the same time you can't *just* say the State system and leave it at that. Some State schools are better than others, and we've tried to find the best in the area. And we've been responsible by example, we've tried to communicate to the kids the kind of concern we feel about society, this is what we're working for, we've said, and we hope you'll work for it too. But again, you can't just say that kind of thing, Adam and Vicky are individuals with their own thoughts to think, their own lives to live. We won't try to influence them about what they do, Adam may turn into a banker, Vicky become a nun.' Charlie gave a brief laugh to suggest the unlikelihood of such futures. This, of course, was before Vicky showed an interest in religion, or before her father knew about it. That must have seemed to him a kind of betrayal, or at least have wounded him. Putting down the sententious phrases makes Charlie sound simply tedious, but there was about him an ingenuousness and even sweetness that made the spoken words less anodyne than they look on the page. I never doubted the depth of his mourning for Vicky, even though it was also for the loss of a soldier in the ranks of progress.

It might be thought that the Sixties would have raised Charlie's spirits. The Profumo scandal, the first and second Wilson Governments, sexual freedom, the rise of feminism, surely he must have approved all these? Yet that wasn't exactly so. Of course he was pleased to see a Labour Government back again, and he waited for the call to an advisory position in relation to Communist Europe, but he waited in vain. Charlie was nearly fifty when the first Wilson Government came to office, and the part he had once played was assumed now by eager young Oxford dons. And he had become oppressed by doubts, like a Victorian cleric. His articles about possible developments in Europe, the problem of Israel and the Middle East, the need for planning in Britain, became so hedged with qualifications that they were in some passages almost unintelligible. A quick sweep through

West Germany and the Soviet satellites plus a visit to Israel, made at Liz's suggestion, did nothing to help. He was much upset when two pieces based on what he had seen in this mini-tour were turned down by the *New Outlook*, and revised versions rejected by *The Times*. And although in theory he was in favour of complete sexual freedom, the anarchic nature of student attitudes appalled him.

'They even argue about what I should teach them, can you imagine? Then they say lectures about the economic basis of society are out of date, they want to discuss Marcuse. I mean to say, *Marcuse*, an infantile anarchist. It's wrong, I tell you, everything's gone very wrong. There's a lot of rethinking to be done.' What sort of rethinking? He was cautious. 'I'm not sure. Perhaps there's been too much planning, too much organisation. It may be a social problem, not an economic one.'

Liz had no such doubts. As the Sixties progressed her career blossomed, extending far beyond that original concern with housing. She became a member of what seemed dozens of organisations, chairperson, as it was called, of some. She served on committees for Council Housing Improvement and Development, Progressive Rating, Planned Energy, Women's Action, Family Aid, New Building structures . . . the list was long. She became even busier and more active, her manner brassily self-confident, every statement she made supported by a quotation from one of the official reports or White Papers piled up in her study. Whenever one visited the house she seemed surrounded by other women, all of them talking in loud high voices. I remember a discussion one day about the problems of people who had been waiting for months and even years to be housed by their local Councils. All sorts of suggestions were made about possible ameliorations of the situation by renovating old houses, making squatting legal, and so on. Liz insisted that there were vacancies. Ah yes, somebody said, but most of them in tower blocks, and Charlie pointed out that they were not just in tower blocks, but mostly on the upper floors, the lifts were often vandalised, one could hardly expect old people or young ones with small children to live on the fifteenth floor—

Liz interrupted him, as she often did in these days. 'People say there are no vacancies. But there are vacancies. Sometimes the lifts don't work, agreed, but we've got teams of engineers to put them right. Then they say oh dear me, no, I don't want to run the risk I might have to climb all those flights of stairs. All right then, if they're so choosy they can join the queue. It will do the British good to learn about queuing.' A youth with hair down his back, one of Charlie's students, asked if she approved of squatters. 'I *understand* squatters', she said with the elaborate patience of a teacher talking to the dullest student in the class. 'I see the reasons. But they cause trouble, make other people angry. They have to be taught to get in line like everybody else.' Her patience ended when the student mentioned the magic name of Marcuse. 'That's all theory, I only know about practice. If Marcuse's books say anything about solving our housing problems perhaps you'll show me the chapters.' The student remained unsatisfied, but Liz's acolytes murmured approval.

With this increased influence and assurance Liz became, perhaps surprisingly, more attractive. The trousers she always wore were exchanged for skirts, with the effect that rather elegant legs were revealed, she began to use scent, an apparent lack of interest in men was replaced by a blend of dominance and coyness which had its charms for some, although not for me. She would be deliberately flirtatious, especially with the French and West German housing experts who had replaced Charlie's East Europeans as visitors to the Paradon home, and then bring them up sharp by saying 'That's nonsense, I have some experience, and let me tell you . . .', the contradiction sounding like a sexual invitation, as if she wished to be taken by force. No doubt that was not the case, for if the argument grew more heated flirtatiousness would disappear altogether, replaced by the dogmatism of the expert. I found this reversal of roles in the Paradon household interesting but distasteful, and saw less of them, particularly after we moved to Romney

Marsh, keeping only a flat in Blackheath. I was alone in this flat one evening when the bell rang, and I found Charlie at the door. He came in, accepted a drink, sat in an armchair and stared at me miserably.

It was a year or more since I had seen Charlie. He might have been wearing the same old clothes, but his appearance had subtly changed. Although his round face and innocent expression were utterly unlike his father's Alf Garnettish air of suppressed anger, something about him reminded me of Dr Paradon. His hair was slipping back, his mouth which had shown an optimistic upward curve now turned down at the corners. I asked what was new. He looked astonished.

'What's new is Czechoslovakia.'

Of course, of course! This was the summer of 1968, Soviet tanks were in the streets of Prague as they had been in Budapest, Communism with Dubcek's human face was in the process of being defeated, Dubcek himself stripped of power. My scepticism about political progress in Communist Europe was so great that I had taken Dubcek's defeat for granted, but I should have realised how much Charlie would be affected by the news. Now he leaned forward, sloshing about the wine in his glass so that a little spilled on the carpet, and spoke earnestly.

'What they've done is unbelievable, you must see that. If they can't accept somebody like Dubcek, what happens to the whole idea of a Socialist state, what's left?'

What was left, I suggested, was Socialist governments in a number of European countries, Sweden, Denmark, Britain—

'You call the Wilson Government Socialist? That ignorant corrupt bureaucracy, staggering from one stupidity to another, don't tell me that has anything to do with Socialism.'

I have said there was a touching innocence about Charlie. There was also, as I have no doubt conveyed, something deeply irritating. On this occasion irritation prevailed, and I said if he felt so contemptuous about the Labour Party he should join the Tories. I also reminded him of Trotsky's reply when

84

confronted with the possibility that he would never see the triumph of Marxism, never see more than continual struggle, constant defeats. He had said in effect that it would then be necessary to salvage what one could from the wreckage, and added: 'Life is beautiful. Let the future generations cleanse it of all evil, oppression and violence.'

Charlie was not cheered by this. He sat sipping his wine and looking at me mournfully. Then he said, 'Adam got a two-one. PPE.' I offered congratulations. 'And a job. In a stockbroker's office. He said the other students at LSE made him sick, the sort of things they said, the way they didn't work, just argued and demonstrated. He thought I should have been tougher with them.' I asked if Adam had been in any of his classes, and he said one or two.

'Perhaps that was a mistake.'

'Perhaps. He told me they laughed at me, said politics ended for me around 1950. It isn't true, I've read Fanon, Marcuse. I don't teach them, what is there to teach, it's all hot air.'

'But Adam's not like that?'

'No. He's got this job, making almost as much as I do already, he says. He thinks of nothing but money. And he's joined the Tories, actually become a Party member, he seemed pleased about it. I think he enjoyed telling me.'

I repressed an impulse to laugh, and said something anodyne about sons rebelling against their fathers, which Charlie ignored. He sat, looking sometimes at me, then at a picture by Julian Trevelyan behind me.

'It's good, that, isn't it? I don't know anything about art, I know that. You've got to specialise, it's better to know a lot about one or two things than a bit about everything. So I've always believed.' This seemed an unprofitable subject to pursue. There was silence. Then he said, 'Liz has gone.'

'Gone?'

'Gone off.'

There flashed into my mind momentarily an image of Liz as a fish, sole or plaice, smelling rather high on the

85

slab. I extinguished the image, and said I was sorry to hear it.

'She's living with Everton Lonsdale.'

I understood then the meaning of those remarks about art. Everton Lonsdale was a trimly bearded dapper little man who lived in Greenwich, and dressed in variously coloured corduroy suits with contrasting bow ties. He had made a reputation in the Sixties as an expert on Pop Art, and could be seen at the Paradons sitting cross-legged on the floor with a group of the young around him as he expounded the merits of Lichtenstein and Warhol, the Beatles and the Rolling Stones, Roger Corman's films, the design of Harlow New Town and Los Angeles. Everton was either a spellbinding conversationalist or a tremendous bore, according to taste, and his conversation was supported by a stream of articles in publications ranging from the *Architectural Review* to the *Daily Mail*. He was certainly no specialist, rather an 'Enquire Within On Popular Art' encyclopaedia. I could see the attraction his style might hold for Liz, although Everton's side of it was not so clear. Perhaps he had got tired of the young women he usually brought to the Paradons, perhaps he wanted a domineering flirt. I hardly knew what to say by way of consolation, except what I believed, that it wouldn't last.

'You don't think so?' Charlie perked up momentarily. 'I've always thought Everton was very superficial, he doesn't know what it's all about. Liz is such a genuine person, she'll see through him.'

It was rather the reverse I'd had in mind, that Everton would get tired of being managed, but I didn't say so. 'Do you know what she said to me? That she'd only been waiting till Adam was off our hands, she'd wanted her freedom for years, she was tired of living with somebody who never made decisions.' I said I should have thought Liz was quite ready to make all the decisions needed. Charlie put up a hand at that, and said he wouldn't hear any criticism of Liz,

86

these things happened, everybody was free to choose, etcetera. He stayed until midnight, repeating similar bromides.

A couple of weeks later Liz rang up and asked me round to supper. 'Nobody else, we can have a good talk.' And so we did, while an aproned Everton darted in and out from the kitchen, producing a much better meal than any I had eaten at the Paradons. Liz, with a new pudding basin haircut that suited her very well, perhaps suggested by Everton, was her usual sharp sensible self. She professed worry about Charlie.

'He's taken it badly, I'm afraid. Trouble is, he just isn't with it any more. Exciting things are happening, but he doesn't want to know.' She began to talk about new building materials, ready-made houses put up in forty-eight hours. I brought her back to Charlie. 'Charlie, yes. Adam's gone, you know that? So Charlie's alone in that great barracks of a place, he won't look after it, he'll be miserable. I wondered about your flat. I mean, you're down in the country most of the time, and Charlie would be much happier there. He'd see you sometimes, he'd like that. And he's really no trouble.' She didn't seem surprised by my firm refusal, merely nodded. 'Something has to be done. I want to sell the house, but it's in both our names. Naturally I'd split the money with Charlie, but he won't agree, won't understand we're finished, washed up. He won't accept reality.' A smiling Everton, divested of apron, brought in the first course. 'I want a divorce, so that Everton and I can get married.' I must have looked surprised. She snapped at me. 'What's so extraordinary? We suit each other.'

'This souffle won't keep', Everton said reprovingly. Liz obediently picked up her fork. He stroked his little beard. 'Liz and I make a true partnership. I don't think that was so of her and Charlie.'

Hadn't it been true? I thought back to those days when Charlie talked and Liz agreed, and knew they would never come again. I said I would speak to Charlie, realising that this was the object of the evening, and later did so with no obvious effect. But Liz was a determined woman, and got her way in the end. Charlie agreed to the house sale, and to a quickie divorce. He moved to Camden Town, where he shared a flat with another man from LSE. Everton sold the Greenwich house, and bought a little place in a part of Pimlico just becoming fashionable. There he and Liz gave parties for visiting academics, administrators of quangos, architects and their potential clients, TV and theatre directors, an occasional rock musician or two, rising politicians of all persuasions.

The social level was perhaps not higher than in Blackheath days, but the composition of the parties was different. 'Their motto is "Let us not to the alliance of a power-hungry couple admit impediments"', Norris Tibbs said. 'Everton's on the Arts Council and a dozen bodies that dispense patronage, Liz is on all the committees that recommend deserving people.' He quoted Roy Campbell: '"Let us commune together, soul with soul, And of our two half-wits compound a whole." Though there's nothing half-witted about Everton and Liz, they're two smooth operators.'

But not Socialists any longer, I suggested. Norris almost choked into his beer. 'Socialists, who said they ever had anything to do with socialism? They're petty bourgeois apparatchiks, froth on the surface of society, that's all.'

And certainly as the revolutionary Sixties merged into the sober Seventies, Everton and Liz Lonsdale kept up with the times. Everton made a stir with a series of articles, 'Where Is Architecture Going?', in which he announced the end of the New Brutalism, said high-rise blocks should be put up only for the rich who knew how to live in them, advocated a blend of styles which he called Renaissance Post-Gothic for public buildings, and Council Cottage Communities for the C to E groups in society. Liz became chairperson of WAWAW (Women Against War And Want), and served on a committee investigating the medical effects of the pill. They had soared into the politico-social empyrean, and I no longer saw them.

I did, however, meet Charlie occasionally. He never recovered from the blow of losing both Liz and Adam (who had joined a merchant bank, married a partner's daughter, and seldom saw his parents), and the deaths of Dr Paradon and Irma in 1972 upset him further. Irma died suddenly of a heart attack, and then her husband was found to be suffering from inoperable cancer. Charlie became after the death of his mother a devoted son, perhaps had always been one. He insisted that his father should come and live in the spare room of the North London flat. Dr Paradon, physically frail but still an angry unforgiving man, upbraided his son for lack of faith, loss of a wife, alienation of a son. 'What have you been in your life, what have you done? Nutting. You are not a Jew, are not a Christian, even got no proper home, just this place, you are nutting. All you teach is wrong, but now you not even do that, I don't know what you do.'

To this Charlie made no reply. It was true that he had taken early retirement from LSE to write a book about what he called the economic infrastructure of the Warsaw Pact countries, and that the book made slow progress and was then abandoned. All this might have been enough to make anybody gloomy, and Charlie's expression became one of permanent wariness, that of a man waiting for the next bad thing to happen. Yet when Dr Paradon died, complaining to the end about the fact that he was compelled to spend his last weeks in a hospice instead of under his son's roof, Charlie was genuinely grieved. There were things he should have done, he said, he had behaved badly to his father.

In spite of these tribulations Charlie perked up with the Heath Government's displacement by Labour in 1974. He was not so optimistic as to think he would be called again to the footstools of the seats of power, but 'You can't *say* that kind of thing' reappeared in his conversation, accompanied by phrases about the need for conforming to an incomes policy, and sticking to the social contract.

It was late in the Seventies that Charlie, his curly poll now almost gone, planned the book that was to revive his reputation. This was a collection of essays by various experienced and youthful figures who supported the Labour movement, politicians, academics and journalists. The basic theme was that, in a current phrase, Labour was the natural party of government, a view based on the fact that, with the exception of the Heath years, Labour had been in power since 1964. Charlie gathered the pieces together, found a publisher, and wrote a long bold introduction asserting that the pragmatic, thoroughly practical policies of the Government showed the way forward for the next decade or more. *Pragmatism: An Idea That Works* was published in the summer of 1979, shortly after the first Thatcher victory at the polls. The jeers with which it was greeted, in the press and elsewhere, may be imagined.

Charlie's troubles never came singly, and this one was in every sense fatal. Not long before the book's publication he went for a check-up, underwent a series of indecisive tests, was rushed to hospital when he collapsed in the street, had a heart by-pass operation that went wrong and within a few weeks (but in time for the book's publication, and the contemptuous reviews) was dead. A black-hatted and suited Liz, and an Everton looking sleeker than ever, came to the funeral, and Liz pronounced her verdict on Charlie.

'He just couldn't cope', she said. 'He was the sort of man who couldn't even get his spectacles mended.'

In the next year's Honours List Liz got a CBE for services to education and housing.

# Mr Jacob the Hairdresser

I HAD MY hair cut in several places during the Fifties and Sixties, all of them handy for the London Library. For a year or two I favoured Simpsons, changed to Austin Reed after some bother about waiting when I had booked an appointment, and when Mr Norman at Austin Reed retired I settled down with Mr Jacob at Malcolm's, in one of the arcades leading off Piccadilly. The 'Mr' was obligatory, one didn't ring and ask for an appointment with Norman or Jacob. Dignity was maintained, perhaps equality asserted. I asked always for Mr Jacob, although when we knew each other he called me Mr S.

Malcolm was a gentle liquid-eyed Italian, who said on my first visit, 'I give you Mr Jacob' as if conferring a considerable favour. Perhaps he was, for Mr Jacob was the busiest of the four assistants, all of them male. There was no unisex hair cutting at Malcolm's.

Mr Jacob was a few years my junior, perhaps in his late thirties. He was of medium height, with a pulpy flexible face rather like that of the late Russell Harty, a fine head of dark hair and brawny, thickly hairy arms. He handled his comb and scissors with style, suggested with a quizzical air that he should take a little off my sideboards, bent low to ask if I would like him to take out the hairs in my ears. I was impressed. The question was new to me, and the sprouting hairs were new also, the products of middle age.

Mr Jacob was not a compulsive talker, but probed delicately for common ground that might provide conversational material. On my second or third visit he struck gold.

'A good week-end, sir?' Quiet, I said, at home, in the garden, peaceful. 'Wish I could say the same. Went to watch the Os, Leyton Orient the proper name, expect you know it if you're interested in soccer. Got beat four nothing, what a shambles.'

The tone was interrogatory, though not the words. Leyton Orient rejected, Mr Jacob might have turned to films, politics, the latest sex scandal. But I rose to Leyton Orient, telling him that a year or two back I had written a book about the swindling financier Horatio Bottomley, and that Bottomley had been a patron of what was then Clapton Orient. I had seen a photograph of him taken with the team.

'Is that so, sir? Very interesting. What might your line be then, sir? I had you down as perhaps a newspaper man.'

A writer of crime stories, I told him, and biographies including that of Bottomley. He punctuated my remarks with little encouraging ejaculations. 'H'm . . . is that so? . . . a real crook he sounds, that Mr Bottomley . . . and you've written about him . . . may I make so bold as to ask, do you come from Hackney or Leyton perhaps . . . ?' He was a little disappointed when I said I was a South Londoner, from Clapham, not Clapton.

But still, the ice was broken. Bottomley was a link between us, Mr Jacob made me as it were an honorary East Ender like himself, and talked freely about his parents who still lived in Leyton, his own home in Stoke Newington, his wife, the absence of children. Before long I became Mr S.

'The old people, you know what it is Mr S, they get set in their ways, what do we want to move for my momma says, I tell her you want to move because it's not far but the air's fresher in Stoke Newington, the air's fresher, you've got Victoria Park, and the houses are better with a nice garden back and front, and you get a different class of people. You think we want to mix with the nobs, she says, here it's not good enough for you? Nah, I say to her, it isn't that, but what's the use of talking, when you're old you're old and that's an end of it. And it's a nice part where you are, Mr

S, is it, Blackheath you say, should be some grass around.'

Foolishly I told him Blackheath was called South London's Hampstead at half the price, foolishly because Hampstead was no more than a name to him, so that the fairly feeble joke lost whatever point it had. Even Piccadilly and the West End were alien territory to him, simply an area where he worked. He came in to work each day by Underground, and the world he knew was not so much wider than that of his parents, an East Londoner's world. I realised the family was Jewish, although Mr Jacob did not say so. That was not his way. Nor did he ask about my own origins, although he obviously wanted to know them. Instead he dropped hints, most of them in relation to food, mentioning lockshen soup, matzos, the way his mother cooked boiled chicken, the richness of the broth. One day I told him my father had been Jewish, my mother not. He affected surprise.

'Is that so, Mr S? You enjoy your bar mitzvah, what an occasion that is.' Nothing like that, I said, I had no religious education of any kind, and in my youth had never even heard of a bar mitzvah. At that he was surprised, perhaps even shocked, although his scissors did not stop snipping, and he made no direct comment. 'The old people, you know what they are, strict, orthodox. Me, I say why not be relaxed, you got to live in the world the way it is my Becky says, and she's right, but what's the use of saying it to the old people? Becky she always wants to have an argument, have it out, but I say why give offence when it's not necessary? Am I right or am I right, Mr S?'

The ice had now been broken in another direction, and Mr Jacob was able to talk freely about Becky, the old people, and a bewildering variety of named cousins, without having entered into details about his family's origins, or even said positively that he had been brought up as an orthodox Jew. I gathered that the old people came from central rather than Eastern Europe, but even that was a matter of inference and deduction, not of statement. It was not until the end of our relationship that I learned his surname, which was Lauscher. He was always Mr Jacob, I remained Mr S.

Within the boundaries of this intimate formality, however, there was a good deal to be said. Not about the way I made a living – from that he metaphorically averted his eyes. I gave him a copy of the Bottomley biography and he thanked me for it, but never referred to it again. Neither he nor Becky, he said, had time for reading, of which he spoke as if it were an optional extra he had considered and rejected.

'Tell you the truth, Becky and me we just don't have the time. Becky she's got this job I told you about with S. Gold and Co, Furriers, very smart man he is Mr Gold, known him since we were kids and his dad set up the shop. He was a decent old gent, but my word, the way Billy's expanded the business you wouldn't know it, went over to Moscow can you believe, did a deal with the Reds, says to me "They may be Reds second, but they're business men first." Sooner you than me, Billy, I said, but you know, I respect him. Whatever way you vote you got to respect success, and look at my Becky, Billy tells me she's the best saleswoman he ever had. "You get them to put it over their shoulders, then you say the right words, they're hooked", Becky says to me. Whether you're selling furs or cutting hair, you got to study human nature, and you don't learn about it from books.'

What about newspapers? 'Never felt the need, nor Becky either. Sometimes she'll buy a woman's paper, one of the classy ones, but that's for the fashion. But you tell me there's been a revolution here, an earthquake there, a shipwreck in the other place, what's it matter to me or Becky either? Will it affect us at number eighty-one Shamwell Road, Stoke Newington? Will our house fall down, will the rates go up? And if I do want to know about it, what do I pay my TV licence for? I tell you, I sit in the Tube in the morning and I see the whole row of 'em with faces stuck in the papers, and I think what a pack of fools. Don't I want to read reports of the O's? Mr S, I *been* to the match, what do I want to *read* about it for? Mind you, if they get to Wembley this season I might just make an exception.' We both laughed at the idea of Leyton Orient reaching Wembley.

It may sound as if our conversations were one-way traffic, but that wasn't so. Mr Jacob was eager to hear details of my life, the house I lived in, whether our children enjoyed school, where we were going for a summer holiday. He was amazed by the size of our house ('Five bedrooms, what an expense, my word your wife must have work to do'), astonished by our employment of an *au pair*. He had, I'm sure, got me marked down as one of his poorer clients, and almost everything I told him was a fresh proof of our household's extravagant wastefulness. But most of our conversation was general, and concerned football in which his interest was passionate. At that time Orient had one of the few talented Jewish players to play professional football, Mark Lazarus, and Mr Jacob was eloquent about the savage barracking Lazarus received at away matches. He also told me something I hadn't realized, that Spurs had the quite undeserved reputation of being a Jewish team. He repeated the fragment of jeering song with which visiting supporters used to greet the Spurs centre forward, Chivers. He leaned over me to whisper the words:

'They asked me how I knew
Chivers was a Jew,
I of course replied
'"Cos he's circumcised"'

I call it disgusting, just persecution, Mr Jacob said, and asked rhetorically whether it was any wonder Jewish boys didn't go in a lot for sport, when that was how they were treated. Why did he go to watch Orient? He'd started at school, going with friends, and had remained faithful, becoming a season-ticket holder. He went to every home match and some of the away games, going to have a meal with the old people after the home matches.

'And what a meal. It's everything I shouldn't have if you get my meaning, first the bean and barley soup, then the chicken with latke or the meat balls. And the schalete, I never eaten anything like my mother's schalete, your wife ever make anything like that?' Never, I said, I didn't even know what schalete was. He didn't tell me (it's a not very exciting apple and raisin cake), but sighed. 'Becky, she doesn't like the way I spend my Saturdays, the season ticket is an expense, she says, why can't I stand the way I used to, I tell her I'm on my feet all day every day, when I go to watch football I want to sit down. And then she doesn't want me eating with the old people, I get the indigestion afterwards, it's bad for me. So it's once every two weeks, I say to her, and she says once is too often, I tell her we should have had kids then she'd have something to worry about. They're the blessing of your life, don't you agree, Mr S, but Becky she wanted to leave it.' I said it surely wasn't too late. In the mirror he paused, clippers in hand, and sorrowfully shook his head.

It was about this time that he sounded warning notes about my hair. In youth this had been as fine a crop as his, and there seemed still a fair amount left when I put a comb through it, but viewed from the front it was visibly slipping back. Could something be done? Yes, Mr Jacob said, if I acted quickly.

'You want a hair weave, and a cousin of mine, he does it.' Hair weaving was at this time a new idea, and he had to explain just what was involved. Then I began to read newspaper stories about the pain involved, infection, times when the weave didn't take. Mr Jacob scouted them.

'It's something new is what you want to remember, something new people always tell you horror stories, they're afraid of it.' He became excited, eloquent. 'I am telling you, Mr S, Morrie is an expert, a real professional, I've seen heads he's done and they're beautiful. Pain, yes, there's a little pain, but think of the result, you look ten years younger. And those infection stories, that only happens when there's dirty needles, and Morrie would never use a dirty needle. With Morrie you're safe, and I will personally guarantee you'd be pleased with the result.' I unwisely made a joke about his enthusiasm being such that he could be a salesman for Morrie. I regretted the words immediately. In the glass his rubbery features took on an injured look.

'Head down.' I bent my head for the shampoo. Powerful fingers raked my scalp, I felt at his mercy. Then the rinse, and my face confronted me again, done up in a towel. 'If that's what you think, so be it. But I'll tell you something. Have it done now, I guarantee nobody will notice, they'll simply say my word, he's keeping his hair well, you take my meaning? Leave it another six months, the way you're losing it—' His hands made a negative gesture. 'Everybody will know. Is that what you want?'

Obviously that was not what I wanted. Was I prepared to spend the money? It would be an exercise prompted by vanity, but then the clothes we wear, the care we take to appear presentable in our own eyes and those of others, the tie knotted with apparent carelessness, the cap worn with conscious bravado, they are exercises in vanity too. For weeks I pondered and dithered, while my hair slipped back. In the end I decided, with regret and relief nicely blended, that it was too late. Mr Jacob returned to the charge occasionally, but not with his former zest. It would be too much to say that rejection of the hair weave created a rift between us, yet things were not quite as they had been. It would again be an exaggeration to say that there was a relationship between us, even though I have used the word already, yet Mr Jacob knew more than most people about my house, my family, the hours I worked. And the glimpses he had given me of his upbringing, his parents, his marriage, were of a kind shown only to friends, or to strangers who are in no position to betray confidences.

There was one revival of the enthusiasm with which he had urged hair weaving on me. As the need for hair-cutting became evidently less, my visits to Malcolm's were less frequent. I came one day in late summer, a little fearfully after a lapse of some weeks, to be greeted by a visibly plumper but bronzed, healthy-looking Mr Jacob with a cheerful, 'Hallo there, you're a stranger.' As we went through the established ritual, stylish hair cutting, shampoo, clipping and trimming, he told me of his first visit to Israel, Becky's reluctance to go with him, his delight that she enjoyed it as much or even more than he.

'Amazing, Mr S, you don't take my advice I know, but I tell you now you must go to Israel, it's a wonderland. In the desert they've made a hundred flowers bloom, it's what they say, and it's true. I tell you, it's a land of milk and honey, I feel I want to weep when I'm at the Wailing Wall, and I don't call myself a religious man. I said to Becky, the first time in my life I really feel at home, and you know what it is, she feels the same way. And it's a land of opportunity, you have a skill you can use it, you don't have a skill but you're ready to learn, they teach you.' I asked, not seriously, if they thought of emigration. 'And why not, what's to stay here for? Becky says to me this job she does selling furs to rich old women, how do you compare it with what we've seen in Israel? I tell you, Mr S, I never thought I'd hear her say such words. Mind you, there's the old people, but they could come out to pay visits.'

Wasn't he on the mature side to emigrate? 'There's older than me, a lot older. And we've saved money, enough so I'd be able to start my own little business, and Becky she's a real saleswoman and they appreciate that, she'd never be out of a job anywhere.' I said he would miss watching the O's, and he took the joke seriously. 'I'll be there Saturday, first match of the season, but still, you got to sacrifice something. Becky, she'll be giving up S. Gold and Co, she liked it there. But first things first.'

The next time I went in to make an appointment, a month later, a new man was using the hair dryer on a client in Mr Jacob's chair. Malcolm came forward to greet me. I said 'Mr Jacob's on holiday? Or has he gone to Israel?'

Malcolm waved elegant hands. 'Mr Jacob has passed away.' I stared at him, unbelieving. 'He goes to the football match, he gets very excited. He has a heart attack, he drops dead. Perhaps you would like to make an appointment with Mr Charles?'

To die watching your favourite football team, I thought, not a bad way to go. I didn't make an appointment with Mr Charles, found another hairdresser. Within a few years I no longer needed one.

# Bert Stubbs
# and Rudi Picabia

I MET BERT Stubbs through my job as secretary and general dogsbody at Victoria Lighting and Dynamo, the small firm where I worked during the Thirties. Among the products we handled was the Puyrelite Lighting fitting, which as the name suggests purported to give an illumination approximating to daylight. There were other daylight lamps and fittings on the market, but Puyrelite was a German product, and as our firm's owner Mr Budette said, everybody knew that something made in Germany was better than a similar article made in England. The egg-shaped fitting, resembling in appearance the once-fashionable Holophane, gave out a dismal blueish light which produced a corpse-like appearance in those near it. Our leaflet about the fitting was accurate in saying it avoided the harsh glare of ordinary electric light, but the claims that it was soothing to the spirit and beneficial to the eyes were, to put it mildly, dubious.

However, the leaflet copy was persuasive, and the technical data looked good. We sold quite a lot of Puyrelites, and some buyers were enthusiastic about their daylight quality, among them a firm named rather grandly The Architectural Designers, whose chief business was in the restoration of old buildings. Their offices were off Victoria Street not far away from us, and I went round there several times to advise on the positioning of the Puyrelites, demonstrate with a light meter their superiority over ordinary fittings, and so on.

The office draughtsmen were less keen about Puyrelite than their bosses, who had swallowed whole the enthusiastic spiel of which Mr Budette was a master. It was at my second visit that one of the draughtsmen said his name was Stubbs, and he had been at school with me. He was three or four years my junior but I remembered him vaguely, a small fair boy who had got a scholarship from our good state school to Battersea Grammar. I realised too that I had known his elder brother Harry, who had played with me for our old boys' cricket team. The younger Stubbs was still rather short, with neat handsome features, carefully brushed fair hair and pale blue eyes. He asked if I ever took sandwiches to eat in St James's Park at lunchtime, and when I said yes asked if he might join me. I was lonely enough to be glad of company, and there was a combination of shyness and assurance about him that interested me. His blue eyes seemed to look wonderingly yet calculatingly at the world around him. As we sat in deck chairs eating our sandwiches he talked dismissively of The Architectural Designers and what he did there.

❁

'*Designers*, that's a joke, we're restorers and you should see what we restore. Modern bay windows put in Georgian houses, mock Tudor timbering and what we call revealed rafters added to Victorian ones, and if there are no rafters to be revealed, never mind, we'll put them in. Architecture used to be called an art, now it's just commerce.'

I have said something elsewhere about that evasive identity, South London speech, and Bert Stubbs had certainly escaped from it. He never said anything like *Sarf* for South, but was inclined rather to the plummy *Sowth*, and the language he used was often untypical of his (and my) background. We both lived in Clapham, and at our second or third sandwich-eating lunch he asked if I would come round one day to meet 'my people', words that neither his brother Harry nor I would have used.

His father was the assistant manager of a bank in Lavender Hill and lived in nearby Lavender Sweep, a road whose dullness belied its romantic name. He was a small man with sharp little eyes peering over glasses that had a tendency to slip down his nose. His wife, whose name I later discovered to be Rose, was twice his size, a brawny Amazon with hair done up in a bun, large features, well-kept white hands on which she wore several rings, and big feet. I had hoped on this teatime visit to see Harry, who had a job as a car salesman, something that when mentioned made Stubbs senior look sour. Harry was out, but Bert's elder sister Bess was there. Since she was a junior model of her mother, and Bert was small like his father, the Stubbs women seemed in command of the men. But this first impression was deceptive. I soon learned that Rose Stubbs was an easygoing accommodating figure, a great maker of puddings and pies, while little Mr Stubbs was master in his home, and could be viperishly unpleasant about a mislaid paper or a forgotten message.

At this first meeting he pecked away at me with questions, with pros and cons mentally noted as I replied. On the *pro* side was the fact that my family lived in a big detached house, that I had what sounded like a secure job (job security then being distinctly desirable), and spoke in a voice that whatever its deficiencies was not that of an obvious South Londoner. *Con* was the fact that I had gone to a state school – without actually asking whether my parents had been unable to afford the fees at Battersea Grammar, Mr Stubbs probed at this problem like a dentist trying to locate a faulty tooth – and perhaps the startling red and green striped shirt I had bought in a sale and was wearing for the first time, plus the stammer which, pretty well conquered in ordinary conversation, emerged under the stress of questioning. In the end Bess said 'Oh, give it a rest, dad'. There was a meaningful glance from those little eyes, but he stopped asking questions. Later Bert took me up to his room and said, on a faintly apologetic note, that his father always liked to have everything cut and dried, whether it was about things or people.

'He likes to know, you see, says you've got to find out where you are with people if you want to get on in the world.

He doesn't want me to be like Harry, a car salesman, what future is there in that?'

I said something about the stupidity of worrying about the future, and he looked surprised. 'I'm going to be some-body, you know, I shan't stay at a drawing board for ever. I thought it might be in architecture, but now I don't know, it seems to be just like any other business.' He waited for a comment, but I said nothing. I was, after all, working in a business, and saw no prospect then of doing anything else. 'Harry told me you write poems, he thought it was a joke. I do too. I'll show you some. Don't look at them now, take them away.' He took a folder from a drawer.

I said being a poet was not what his father meant by getting on in the world, and he agreed. 'I know. But if you become really famous it's all right. Like Tennyson, he was made Lord Tennyson.' There were a couple of shelves of books in his room, among them volumes of Keats, Tennyson, Rossetti, as well as some anthologies. Otherwise the room was impersonal, no photographs by the bed or on the walls, everything neat, tidy, and blank of individuality as a hotel room. I asked if he was looking for a different kind of job, since he didn't like what he was doing.

'I don't mind it for the time being. It's useful, you're learning about life, what people are like. I'm waiting for something to happen, so are you. You're going to be somebody like me, most people are just nothing. Like dad. He knows he's nothing, that's why he's always asking questions.'

This was said without the least trace of feeling. When I got home I read the poems. I don't know what I expected, but it was something other than the washed-out imitations of nineteenth century romanticism I found, full of beauteous damsels, rose red lips, that great orb the sun, and furled-curled rhymes. At lunch in the park I gave them back and said they weren't my cup of tea.

'You mean they're no good. Why not?' I said something about outdated language, and may have used the word cliché. 'So you mean, to write poetry you've got to be up-to-date. Yes,

I understand that.' He took the poems from the folder, tore them across, and dropped them into a handy bin. He shook his head when I said he should have shown them to somebody else. 'You say the language is wrong, that means the poems are no good. I understand if you want to write you've got to be up-to-date, so it's been useful. Thanks, don't worry about it. I've decided I shan't be an architect, I'll be a writer, it's just a matter of learning.' I felt that in spite of his words he really didn't understand why the poems were null.

Dismissal of them made no difference to our relationship. It fell short of friendship, but there was an assurance about Bert Stubbs that impressed me. Almost all adolescents are vulnerable, prone to awful emotional or social gaffes that keep them awake at night, but he seemed immune to such feelings. He made mistakes, sometimes of an elementary kind like pronouncing *Freud* to rhyme with *brood*, but remained unembarrassed when they were pointed out, and never repeated them. His relations with his parents were cool, not as the word is used now nor in the sense of being distant, but simply lacking emotion. He told me his father was a failure because he came from a family with money, took a good degree at Christ Church, but then didn't make use of the acquaintances he had made and the opportunities open to him, and so ended up as an assistant bank manager in the suburbs. When I asked if he had wanted to go to university himself he said it would have been no use to him. It occurred to me that the family might have lacked money to send him, but he spoke with an assurance that put such considerations out of mind.

The assurance was not accompanied by any particular intellectual power or subtlety. It was with Bert Stubbs and a couple of other people that I saw my first Marx Brothers film, UFA films, *The Testament of Doctor Mabuse*. He laughed dutifully at *Animal Crackers*, agreed the German films were unusual, but waited on the reactions of the rest of us before expressing an opinion. It wouldn't be right to say he slavishly followed the views of others, rather that he was concerned to find out whether seeing films was really worth the time involved. I never heard him say in the presence of other people that he was going to be somebody.

A few months later he left The Architectural Designers for another firm of architects in North London and I lost touch with him, though he remained in my mind as an enigmatic rather than a colourless personality. His sister Bess who walked out with and later married a member of our cricket team named Johnny Poolman, a clerk in Wandsworth Council, agreed with me.

'He's not like other people, Bert. He only thinks about himself.' She was less critical than admiring. 'He told me about you not liking his poems. He said you might be right now, but he'd show you you were wrong one day. Do you know what he's doing now, you'll never guess.' I guessed he had set up on his own as an architect. She shook her head. 'He's in a bookie's office. He says you must have money if you're going to amount to anything, and if you've got any intelligence you ought to be able to make some quickly working for a bookmaker. Dad's very upset.'

I told her what Bert had said about a university being no use to him, and she laughed. She laughed often and gustily, showing splendid teeth and a pink gullet. She was a hearty open girl, quite unlike her younger brother.

'He was kidding you. Kidding himself as well. He longed to go to Oxford, nowhere else would do, but there was never any question of it.' Because Stubbs senior couldn't afford it? 'I think dad might have managed it somehow, but Bertie's not all that clever, you know.' I suggested that he might have had in mind that his father was at Oxford, never made use of his degree and lost contact with his friends there. She stared at me. 'Is that what he said, dad went to Oxford? I told you Bertie was a kidder, he can't help it. Dad was born and brought up in Birmingham, went to a grammar like Bertie, then straight into a bank. If he's ever been to Oxford it was on a day trip in a chara.' She returned to her brother's abilities. 'He never did anything special at Battersea Grammar, just run of the mill like me. Not like me, though, because he's bright.'

A gusty laugh. 'But not really clever. He just wants to be a success, and if you want something enough you usually get it. He's not to be called Bert or Bertie any more, says it's a silly name, it's Roger now. That's his second name, he's Albert Roger Stubbs.'

It was Bess who kept me in touch with Bert's or Roger's up-and-down career in the years before the War. He made some money with the bookmaker, set up on his own as A. R. Stubbs, Turf Accountant, went broke because of an accumulation of bad debts, worked for an estate agent, briefly as an encyclopaedia salesman, and – more significantly in the light of later events – as agent for a line of fine art reproductions marketed in Britain by an Italian firm. This was the low point of his career, which took an upward turn when he got a job on the *Daily Express*. He had a by-line before long as Roger Stubbs, and wrote for the most part facetious pieces about things like sausage-eating contests and bathing-belle competitions with occasional ventures on to more serious ground, like a review of the Royal Academy's annual exhibition with special attention to what were then still called problem pictures.

I can date our next meeting, if not exactly, to a particular year and month. For three weeks in June 1936 an International Surrealist Exhibition was held at the New Burlington Galleries in Bond Street. It is a mark of British insularity that this was the first time many of us had seen a Surrealist picture. Most of the press treated the show with hilarity ('More laughable than Charley's Aunt'), but to a good many young writers and painters it was astonishing, a revelation. My friend Ruthven Todd went to it every day, and made himself useful around the show. He was rewarded, not with much money, but with a little drawing Picasso gave him, signed and inscribed 'a Monsieur Ruthven Todd'. Ruthven kept it for some years and then it vanished, sold no doubt to pay the most pressing of his multifold debts. He was always fascinated by anything new. I was fascinated too, but only momentarily. Within a few months I was calling Surrealism a movement of literary painters and saying it had 'no standards of craftsmanship but automatic standards', remarks that still seem sensible.

That is by the way. To the point is the fact that when paying a second visit to the exhibition and looking at a picture by Miro full of brightly coloured blobs and squiggles, I heard my name spoken. I turned, and there was Bert or Roger Stubbs, distinctly changed but instantly recognisable, a butterfly emerged from the chrysalis. He wore a blue suit with a dashing red stripe, a tie matching the stripe, and highly polished black shoes.

He spoke with characteristic certainty about the exhibition. Magical, he said, these were magical paintings that took us into another universe, transformed the dullness of daily life but still kept the materials of that life, cigarettes, bits of paper, old tins and bottles. It sounded to me as if he was quoting from an article he had read or perhaps was preparing to write, and not without malice I asked if he was reviewing the show for the *Express*.

'They wouldn't take it seriously. I'm doing it for . . .' He mentioned an art magazine I had never heard of.

'You're quoting your own review.'

'Of course, why not?' He seemed pleased to see me, as I found I was to see him. We went out for coffee. He produced a long amber cigarette holder, lighted up, asked what I was doing. 'You're not still with that potty little engineering company?' When I said yes he raised his eyes to look at the ceiling, and blew a smoke ring. The absence of comment was eloquent. I said I'd heard news of him through Bess, and he said his sister was a sweet girl but would never get anywhere married to a council clerk, any more than Harry would working for pin money plus a commission.

'Perhaps she doesn't want to get anywhere, perhaps she's happy as she is?' He sipped his coffee, and again didn't bother to comment. 'Just as your father was content to take a job in a bank when he left school. You told me he was at Christ Church and got a good degree.'

A desire to puncture his assurance was no doubt responsible for the way I said this. It was not successful. He tapped the ash off his cigarette, which I noticed was a Balkan Sobranie, and said 'He's dying, you know. Cancer. The doctor says six months. Mum's awfully upset.'

I said Bess hadn't told me, he asked how long it was since I'd spoken to her, and nodded when I said a few weeks. 'He only learned a fortnight ago. Dad's always wanted me to be a success, now it looks as if it will be a near thing whether he sees it or not.' No doubt I looked my bafflement. 'My novel. I thought Bess would have mentioned it, *The Cage of Being*. Mallet and Chisell are doing it, it will be out sometime in the autumn.'

I wondered how much of this was true, whether peppery little Mr Stubbs really had cancer or that had been Bert's instant invention, designed to avoid admitting he had lied about his father's background. And did the novel exist outside his imagination? I asked what it was about.

'I suppose you might say the usual thing, the problem of being somebody in the twentieth century, and making sure what you are. Remember you said I was no good at poetry? Of course you were right, that was helpful.' I began to say *no good at poetry* wasn't really what I'd said, but he went on. 'I met Charles Mallet when I was selling his *Encyclopaedia of Everyday Living*. I daresay you think I was stupid to try and sell encyclopaedias, and you'd be right in one way, very wrong in another. Right because it was desperately hard work getting orders, wrong because going from door to door you find out what people are like. And what you're like yourself, you see into the whole cage of being. If I'd not done the rounds with those encyclopaedias I might have got the *Express* job but I'd never have held on to it, and I'd never have written the novel. Charles says it's bound to be a tremendous success.'

The novel was real enough. It came out that November, but didn't fulfil Charles Mallet's prediction. I saw two or three reviews using words like 'immature' and phrases like 'a young man's novel'. I borrowed Bess's copy, which was inscribed 'To Bess, from her brother the author'. It was about a young painter of unrecognised genius, who did badly-paid commercial work to keep alive. He married, had a child, threw up the commercial work in disgust, his wife left him and took the child, the dealer who had been handling his work gave it up as hopeless, he starved, caught pneumonia and died. The preface and postscript were about the immensely successful exhibition put on after the painter's death, and the penitence of all concerned.

I was disconcerted, as I had been with the poems, by the romantic slushiness of the plot and writing, which seemed out of key with Bert's character. (I still thought of him by that name.) Yet in a way I was impressed. He was not a youthful prodigy like David Gascoyne, who published a novel when he was seventeen, but he was in his early twenties when the book appeared.

So the novel existed. The story about his father's illness had a factual basis too, though one much embroidered, since the trouble was a gastric ulcer. This kind of embroidery, laughing Bess said, was what you learned to expect from Roger, there was always a basis of fact in what he said, but it was rarely the exact truth. Probably he had invented Mallet's enthusiastic words, and she suggested he might have paid something towards the book's publication, asking if that was possible? I said it was possible. Mallet and Chisell was a small firm, went out of existence with the War, and may have asked some of their authors to pay part of the cost of publication.

A few months later Bess produced Billy, the first of four children, and invited me to what she said would be a scrap supper on Boxing Day, eating up bits of turkey. I arrived to find a family party, gimlet-eyed little Mr Stubbs looking more withered and Rose more like an overblown flower than they had in the past. Harry was there, wearing a check suit and with only two subjects of conversation, the largely imaginary cricketing triumphs of our youth and his perhaps equally imaginary triumphs in selling cars. Johnny's loud-voiced publican father and his mousy wife, along with Johnny himself, made up the party.

All exclaimed over the beauty and gurgling charm of Billy. The scene was Dickensian, or perhaps only Priestleyan, mistletoe in the hall, a blazing fire, the room thick with paper decorations looped round pictures and paper Chinese lanterns hanging from the ceiling, Rose and Bess dashing in and out of the kitchen, and Billy being passed from lap to lap like a parcel, until the parcel began to leak and smell and was removed for changing. At half-past six Mr Stubbs took out his fob watch and asked where Bertie was, at seven Rose was saying no need to worry because the pudding wouldn't spoil, at seven-thirty Bess that something urgent must have come up at the paper, and jovial Mr Poolman that he felt his tummy rumbling. Billy had been put down, gone through a shrieking period and fallen into sound sleep.

At eight o'clock we ate, cold turkey and ham and the jellied meat dish now vanished called Suffolk cheese, a hot meat pie brought by Rose, hot potatoes, potato salad, Russian salad, mild and hot pickles, cranberry sauce and red currant jelly. There was beer for the men, port and lemon for the ladies. The main course had been disposed of, and we were eating Rose's Christmas pudding and mince pies accompanied by cream and brandy butter, when Bert arrived.

He ate only a token mince pie, saying he was not hungry. Mr Stubbs was inclined to make an issue of this, but Rose shushed him. Then it was presents time. He had come in carrying a gigantic teddy bear for Billy and a bagful of other gifts. He had obviously been forewarned about the company and had brought presents for everybody, a pipe for his father and a crocodile handbag for Rose, a gold-plated Waterman pen for Bess and a gilt-edged leather wallet for Johnny, a cigarette lighter inside a model Rolls Royce for Harry, a couple of cigars in metal cases for Mr Poolman and chocolates for his wife. There was even a gift for me, a copy of the *Golden Treasury* on India paper, in which he had written 'From Roger, who stopped writing poems on your advice.'

When the presents had been exclaimed over and his own rather indifferent gifts accepted (a tie, a pair of pyjamas, a box of Balkan Sobranies, nothing from the senior Poolmans or from me), Mr Stubbs was no longer to be denied.

'We waited supper.' Bert said he was sorry. 'There are such things as telephones, I suppose. I thought you often used one in your office. I don't know what you can have been doing at that paper so important you couldn't telephone. Not when you think of all the rubbish they print.'

Bert never had much colour, and this evening was markedly pale. 'I've left the paper.'

His father echoed the words disbelievingly. Rose said nothing, simply looked at her son. Harry said 'Been asked to advise the government about newspapers, I'll bet', and Poolman senior made a joke about cancelling the *Express*. Bess asked when he'd left, at which he made an irritated gesture and said weeks ago. Then she asked what he was doing now. Still with that air of intense irritation he said he had set up in business with a friend. His father took over again.

'What friend is that? Do we know him?'

'His name is Scott, I met him when I was on the paper.'

'And what sort of business?'

'Scott has contacts in Germany, Hungary, Czechoslovakia. We're agents for several firms there, we import fancy goods.'

'*Fancy goods*', Mr Stubbs said. 'And what are they, pray?'

'Anything from glassware, the Czechs are very good on that, to mirrors, special toilet sets, all sorts of children's toys. For God's sake what is this, I thought it was a party.'

I could see Mr Stubbs was brim full of further questions, but Rose hushed him and said we'd waited for Roger to pull the crackers. So they were pulled, and paper hats put on, and we played party games, hunt the thimble and charades and a game called Continuities, and Bert seemed cheerful but a bit abstracted, as if he was thinking about something else.

As no doubt he was. Three months later I heard from Rose that he'd been arrested on a charge of fraud or embezzlement, she wasn't sure which. No doubt problems had been looming up for him at Christmas and, in a way typical of him, he had tried to dispel or forget them by producing all those presents as a guarantee to us and himself that he was doing well. I never found out exactly what had happened, or whether he'd left the *Express* voluntarily or been sacked. So far as I gathered from reading the case in the papers, the agencies held by Scott and Stubbs had been perfectly genuine and the goods readily saleable, but Scott, or Bert, or both of them, had siphoned off a lot of the proceeds and produced false accounts. Scott disappeared and Bert took the rap, which was an eighteen months sentence. Whether he was guilty, or a victim of the villainous Scott as Bess fiercely claimed, I never found out.

That was the last I saw of Bert Stubbs for a long time. With the threat and then the actuality of war my own life changed. I lost touch with the people I knew in Clapham, was inducted into the army and invalided out of it. I ran across Bess a couple of times, once before the blitz on London began, then when I was in barracks at Catterick and met her in Richmond, our local drinking town. She had moved out of London when the bombing became fierce, along with what were now three children, and gone north to Yorkshire instead of west to the more usual counties for evacuees, Devon and Cornwall. Her mother was living with her in a village outside Richmond, her father had died of a heart attack in the first year of the war. Harry had volunteered when the War began, and been killed during the retreat to Dunkirk. I asked hesitantly about Bert, that is, Roger.

'He's a lieutenant in the FSP, the Field Security Police. The last I heard he was in Italy.'

The FSP, dedicated to discovering and checking any signs of disaffection in the armed forces, occupied a high place in the demonology of Left-wingers like me. I was surprised, not that Bert should have taken on such a job for he had never shown any sign of political interest or feeling, but that somebody with a criminal record should have been accepted. Bess said she thought he still had important friends at the *Express*, people who knew he was innocent. She believed one of them, perhaps Tom Driberg, had spoken to Lord Beaverbrook. Was there some backstairs influence at work? Since Driberg was a well-known homosexual, this made me wonder at the time about Bert's sexual orientation, which when I knew him best I would have called neuter. Soon after the war ended I met somebody who had been in the FSP, and learned that Major Roger Stubbs had ended up on Alexander's staff.

❁

The years after the war saw a flowering of British art in the neo-Romanticism of Minton and Craxton, the dandyish aestheticism of Cecil Collins, the decaying black monsters of Francis Bacon, the austerity of Colquhoun's doomed harlequins and grey harridans, the hard accuracy of Michael Ayrton's portraits. These were all more or less figurative artists, but there were other native forces at work, forces later claimed to be precursors of Abstract Expressionists like Motherwell, and Pop Artists like Johns and Rauschenberg. (As it may be claimed with justice that Rayner Heppenstall's novels anticipated the French *nouveau roman*.) These anti-figurative artists called themselves Immaterialists, Simultaneists or Post-Orphists. A few of their pictures could be seen at the Leicester Gallery, Freddy Mayor's or Roland Browse and Delbanco, but their true home, and the place where several of them made their first appearance, was the Picabia Gallery.

This gallery was one of the unlikely success stories of the Fifties. It was in the wrong place for a start, in Pimlico instead of fashionable Bond Street, and it was a converted greengrocer's shop, with a newsagent on one side and a laundrette on the other. This was not a piece of eccentricity on the part of the gallery's owner Rudi Picabia, the choice of place prompted by the fact that the gallery had been started on a shoestring. No doubt it was for the same reason that the first exhibition was of the group of British artists who called themselves Immaterialists.

Since the Immaterialist movement belongs to the past, perhaps the paraphrase of a fragment from a little out-of-print book called *What Is Immaterialism?* may be useful. Immaterialism was a belief in the artistic value of what is *not there*, so that an Immaterial picture of a pair of boots without laces would be a painting of the laces alone, perhaps called 'Pair of Brown Boots, size 9, made by De Vries, without laces'. The perfect immaterial work would be one not painted, emphatically not there. A number of recent paintings which are pure white or black, with perhaps the faintest hint of a streak of another colour, approach the Immaterial ideal. They hang in museums while Immaterialism is forgotten by all except art historians, although it seems no less plausible as an idea than currently fashionable Conceptualism, to which it shows some similarity.

This by way of background. The Immaterial exhibition received a lot of press attention, and in those terms at least was a success. When it was followed by a show of the young artists who called themselves Simultaneists (their work bearing a resemblance to that of Futurists like Balla and Carra), and then a group exhibition of Immaterialists, Simultaneists and Post-Orphists, the Picabia Gallery was firmly on the map as a place where you would find the really up-to-date thing at what one critic called bargain basement prices. The fact that it was easily accessible, yet oddly situated for an art gallery, was an added attraction. And Picabia was not concerned only with the modern. He discovered a Victorian naive painter, a Lancashire mill hand named William Holder, whose mid-century pictures of dark Satanic mills and those who worked in them received as much critical praise as the equally crude seascapes of the Cornishman Alfred Wallis had done two or three decades earlier. The Holder exhibition sold out in a week.

It was some three years after the gallery had been launched that, after calling on a friend in Pimlico's St George's Square,

I walked up Lupus Street and went into the gallery, attracted by a picture in the window called 'The Nightmare', which contradicted the title by showing in true Immaterialist style two picnickers under a cloudless sky. At the top left hand of the picture the word 'Night' was printed, at the bottom right 'Mare'. The artist was Charles Redmayne, one of the better-known Immaterialists.

Inside the door I was approached by one of those tall elegant perfectly-coiffed blondes (they are sometimes brunette) who seem indigenous to art galleries. She asked if I didn't find 'The Nightmare' terribly amusing, handed me a price list which made it clear that the bargain basement had turned into Harrods, and was turning away when a figure emerged from a back room, said 'Evelyn, will you ring the printer about—' and then paused, so that she said 'About the catalogues, Mr Picabia?' on an interrogative note. It was Bert Stubbs.

He had known me, and I had recognised that voice with its overlay of culture on the South London base. I found myself caught in a continental embrace carrying a whiff of aftershave or cologne, then led into an office and offered a selection of drinks from a cabinet. Here everything seemed made of black glass, the big desk and its fitments, two lamp standards and a chandelier from which black glass petals dangled, everything except the chromium and black leather chairs. Over a glass of sherry I considered the man who was now Rudi Picabia. He had changed, but for the better. Wings of grey hair gave him a 'man of distinction' look, his face had filled out yet the lines had hardened, so that he appeared formidable rather than innocent. He now had the presence and air of a successful West End actor, of a kind then being replaced by earthy and deliberately uncouth figures like Albert Finney. He laughed when I asked him why Bert or Roger Stubbs had turned into Rudi Picabia.

'Remember the Surrealist exhibition, how I said the pictures were magical? That's what I want to show here. For me a picture must be magical, but it should also be fun.' I seemed to have read the phrase in an interview. 'And who was a greater funster than Picabia? You know he once made a portrait out of pen nibs, curtain rings and blotting paper? And the poem he made up about Cezanne's painting which ended "It bores me stiff"? And then he called a book a bhooq, b-h-o-o-q, which I liked. So I thought there couldn't be a better name for a gallery.'

'And Rudi?'

'It seemed to go with Picabia.' I said the gallery had been very successful, and he didn't deny it. 'Remember when I was young I said I was going to be somebody. And you've made a bit of a name for yourself too.'

The condescension implied annoyed me. I said it wasn't easy to compare a writer with the owner of a picture gallery, and that he'd made some boss shots before hitting the target. He was not discomposed.

'It's a matter of finding what to do, what you're fitted for, then doing it.' Again I sensed the background of an interview in *Harper's* or *Vogue*. 'Remember those poems I showed you? And the novel I wrote, did you ever read it? Kid's stuff, I didn't know what I was doing. But mistakes are worth making if you learn from them.' He seemed likely to go on in this vein. I checked him by asking who had put up the money to start the gallery. He leaned forward, his voice lowered to a vibrant whisper.

'*Nobody* put up any money. People I approached said I was crazy wanting to put on a show of unknown British artists, I told them British Is Best. The bank gave me a loan, that was all, and everything went according to my game plan.' He ticked off points on well-shaped fingers. 'With the first show you go for publicity, doesn't matter whether it's friendly or not. To tell the truth, that Immaterialist exhibition got a lot of notice, but not much sold after it. But you build on the publicity, and once you've had a success you find the pictures down in the cellar begin to sell too.'

'And then there was Holder.'

'Then there was Holder' he agreed, adding in a neutral

tone more irritating than obvious complacency, 'The master stroke. I spotted two in a Preston junk shop, then searched for any descendants, and eventually found this great-grandson. He had more pictures on the wall, later on found some in an attic – and there was a unique Victorian painter. Now the great-grandson's unearthed some more, there'll be another Holder show in the autumn, and the prices are going through the roof. I've got American collectors and museums queuing up.'

We talked for half an hour or more. I had always felt Bert was close to his mother, but Rudi Picabia spoke of her death a couple of years back without emotion. She had suffered, he said, from a rare variety of bone cancer, and had wasted away so that big gusty Rose weighed less than six stone when she died. It was at her funeral that he had last seen Bess, still the wife of a clerk in Wandsworth Council. 'I believe he's risen to be assistant Finance Officer or something like that', he said with the trace of a smile. 'But really we don't have much in common.'

Was there anybody with whom he did have much in common? That unspoken question seemed to be answered when the room was invaded by a woman whose face I vaguely recognised, a recognition not unlikely because I learned later that she was the divorced wife of the Earl of something or other, a great party-giver, her name and photograph often in gossip columns and magazines. She came in with a swirl of skirts and the step and style of an aristocratic mare, bringing a dash of Mayfair into Pimlico. There was an exchange of kisses, rapid volleys of glottal-stopped speech, then 'Don't forget it's dinner with the Shashas tonight' (*Shashas* was the way it sounded) and she was gone, leaving no doubt that Rudi Picabia had shed for ever the skin of Bert Stubbs.

The enigmas of personality must hold particular interest for a writer of crime stories, who creates and solves puzzles, and the problem of Rudi Picabia fascinated me. I know, of course, that it could be called a problem of my own making, solved simply enough by saying he had always wanted to 'be something' in the world, and in the end succeeded. Yet that ignored a part of him that, as I saw it, held no element of calculation and might be called naive. The impulse that led him to write poems and a novel was not simply a desire for fame. He wanted to succeed, but also to show an aesthetic judgement he did not possess. The Picabia Gallery was thus a double triumph, bringing not only fame and money, but justification of his artistic sense. The art movements he introduced and publicised might be ephemeral but critics took them seriously, and when he said the discovery of William Holder was a master stroke he meant his artistic sense had been acknowledged.

This is a charitable reading, and charity in relation to Rudi Picabia soon became in short supply.

The Holder exhibition was scheduled to open in November, and in August one of the Sunday colour magazines published a piece about it, including an interview with Rudi, another with the great-grandson Jeremiah Holder in which he told of discovering the new pictures in the possession of a recently deceased uncle, and reproductions of three pictures, a landscape, a mill scene with workers going home, and a portrait thought to be the artist's wife.

A couple of weeks later another Sunday paper printed an article written by what was called their 'Arts Research Team' headed: 'The New Holders, Are They Genuine?', and saying that several details in the mill scene and the landscape had not existed in Holder's lifetime. The piece in the following week: 'William Holder, A Hoax on the Art World' was the killer punch. The Arts Research Team had found a picture restorer who said paintings signed 'Wm Holder' had been brought to him, he had been asked if he could produce similar work, and had said they were very bad paintings but he could do something like them. He had then produced a number of paintings and signed them 'Wm Holder', including the three reproduced in the colour magazine.

The restorer, a genial character named William Blake, roared with laughter as he told this to the Arts Research

Team: 'Mind you, I couldn't paint that bad. Mine were a lot better.' He had worked from photographs, and if the new pictures had things in them that shouldn't have been there it was because the photographs were the wrong date. He had been paid fifty pounds a time for small Holders, eighty pounds for bigger ones. Did he know they'd fetched ten times that much and more? He was philosophical. 'I reckon I got a fair whack, no complaints. As for what they'll fetch, there's one born every minute.'

Who had brought him the paintings and photographs? The gentlemen who came never gave names, but he identified Jeremiah Holder as the man who asked him to produce new pictures, and Rudi as a later visitor who had asked him to confirm that the pictures were genuine. 'I give him a wink and said of course they're genuine. And so they were, genuine William Blakes.' The paper printed an interview with Rudi, in which he admitted consulting Mr Blake, asking his advice as an expert picture restorer, and engaging him to clean and restore some of the pictures, but denied the rest.

There was a third article, 'The Holder Fraud, The Damning Facts', in which Jeremiah Holder admitted that only the junk shop pictures and one or two others were genuine. Was it true, as he claimed, that the London dealer who had astonished him by saying these were valuable paintings knew that most of the others in the first show, and all in the projected second, were fakes? Or did that passion for making the right artistic judgement inherited by Rudi Picabia from Bert Stubbs allow him to deceive others by first fooling himself? That is what I should like to believe, but will never know. On the day the third article appeared Rudi hanged himself from the black chandelier in his office. It was an end Francis Picabia, the genuine Picabia it might be said (but what is *genuine* or *false* in matters of personality?), would have approved. In dreams I sometimes see Rudi hanging from the chandelier, the black glass petals obscuring his face.

# The Vision of
# Norris Tibbs

THE NAME OF Norris Tibbs has cropped up
in two or three of these sketches, and he plays a major
role in this last one. For more than twenty years, from
the late Thirties onwards, Norris was the literary editor of
that archetypal Socialist weekly *The New Outlook*. It used to
be said of the *New Statesman*, in those decades when its circulation was high and its influence allegedly considerable, that
there was no communication between the front and back ends
of the paper, and that few people read both. The front end
of the pantomime horse was political, the back end artistic,
and in the Thirties and Forties the back legs 'embodied the
Bloomsbury spirit' as V. S. Pritchett put it, in a way often
out of step with the front. When Pritchett replaced Raymond
Mortimer as literary editor the gap was less noticeable, but
it grew to the width of the Mississippi when Paul Johnson
became editor and the back end was in the hands of Karl
Miller.

That is by the way, said only to contrast the *New Statesman* of
those days with the *New Outlook*, which was a frankly political
paper acknowledging, sometimes reluctantly, the existence of
the arts. The editor, VR, was said to call all the members of
the Cabinet – that is, the Labour Cabinet – by their Christian
names. He also claimed that they all read it and took notice
of the policies it advanced, which might roughly be called
militantly Left-wing but anti-Communist. VR was a tough
journalist who had come to the paper from the *Daily Herald*,
and was interested only in politics and soccer. His politics,
as he said, were practical and not theoretical, and he was

more interested in the fine print of British politics than in American presidential battles or the internecine struggles in European countries, hence the departure of Elsie Smith from the paper. The soccer team he supported was the eminently pragmatic Arsenal, rather than what he called the flim-flam football of Chelsea and Spurs. The pages given to the arts represented VR's acknowledgement that they existed, and had to be noticed. I am sure he felt the space could have been filled better by articles about the growth of comprehensives or (after the Tories took office in 1951) the iniquities of various Tory policies.

As literary editor Norris was VR's perfect complement. He too was a Socialist, a Labour Party member since his mid-teens and for some years a committee member of the NUJ. But Norris, as I mentioned earlier, regarded Philistinism in relation to the arts as the inevitable price that must be paid for the benefits of Socialism. It was no surprise to him, and indeed justified such beliefs, when VR complained about a leading article on Coleridge. Norris saw himself as fighting battles that could never be won, and his relationship with VR might be called one of friendly animosity. At the weekly policy meetings he complained about lack of space, and occasionally won more for a particular book or a special issue. VR on his side sometimes slapped down a poem he found unintelligible or what he called an airy-fairy review. On such terms they co-existed contentedly, drinking in different pubs, Norris in the Plough off Chancery Lane, VR mostly in the Devereux or the George.

Norris was small and dark with a neat handsome head, as a drinker not speedy, but putting me in mind of Ransom's lines:

> A better man was Aristotle,
> Pulling steady on the bottle.

Drink makes most people loquacious, but generally had the opposite effect on Norris. He became less talkative as he downed beer after beer, offering only occasional witty remarks about contemporary novelists and poets. Or perhaps they only seemed witty to senses oiled by drink. 'When Auden landed in New York he should have told the customs: "I have nothing to declare but the loss of my genius" . . . Henry Green mistakes inarticulateness for art . . . Ivy Compton-Burnett is an Agatha Christie for the intellectuals . . . unalloyed success means ultimate failure . . . English writers wear their ignorance like a coat of armour . . .' I'm afraid the phrases may not look as good on the page as they sounded in the semi-darkness of the Plough.

I suppose the average length of a literary editor's tenure is about five years, after which they have a row with the proprietor or the editor and resign, or decide to move on to richer financial pastures. But Norris stayed through the War (he had asthma, and was rejected for military service), through the six years of the post-war Labour Government and the Tory regimes that followed. And, as those occupying a position for a long time tend to do, he turned into a legend, a man fighting a weekly battle between artistic beliefs and Socialist principles in which the artistic beliefs mostly came out on top. He was the incorruptible hero who somehow managed to square the circle of Socialist populism and the minority values of modernism. Did Mortimer and Pritchett (to name no others) face similar problems? Not exactly, for they were not, like Norris, militant Socialists. Norris strove for the triumph of Socialism, but struggled to nourish just those tender sprouts that full-blooded Socialism was likely to bury underground. As the years went by even VR acknowledged the nobility of Norris's battle, and when he retired after a heart attack so did his successor, an amiable MP named Joss Bedford.

I may have made Norris sound a reclusive figure, but that would be almost the reverse of the truth. On the contrary he was almost too easily accessible, the door of his triangularly-shaped office at the paper always open, his readiness to let reviewers take away books at times almost embarrassing.

When the review came in, however, he was not at all indulgent. At his table in the Plough he would tell reviewers that they had produced slack, carelessly written work that ignored the values of literature and said more about themselves than their ostensible subject. He was kinder-hearted, or perhaps less sure of himself, in relation to original work like poems and short stories. So far as reviews were concerned he never relaxed his standards, or let the demands of friendship affect the choice of reviewer. Indeed, I don't think he was aware that friendship might involve any such demands. One of the part-time assistants he was allowed to enlist, when under Joss Bedford he was given more pages, came to him in tears when she read in proof a review I had written about a collection of poems by one of her friends. Norris listened to this pretty Cambridge Leavisite, then asked her to sit down, telephoned me, repeated the objectionable phrases in the review which were something like 'technically inept and emotionally null', and asked me to justify them. I said the quotations I had given in the review were enough justification. 'You don't want to change anything?' Norris asked in his precise voice, and when I said no told the pretty girl the review would have to stand. She left the office still weeping, and I believe never came back.

Characters like Norris accumulate round themselves, not by their own volition, a crust of fantasy. He appeared to have no existence outside the paper, arriving punctually at ten o'clock each morning, leaving soon after midday for the Plough, returning from the pub at three, leaving the office at six or later except on press days, when he spent the afternoon at Hounslow with the printers. He occasionally went out to dinner nearby with someone from the office, but attended no literary parties, and seemed immune to the admiration of Leavisite girls or spectacled young men from red brick universities. There were admirers even among politicians, even or perhaps especially after he rejected a review by an ex-Cabinet minister on the ground that it was only semi-literate, but he seemed equally indifferent to them. He had many acquaintances but no friends. He was said to live in Hammersmith, but nobody I knew had been invited to his home. Among the rumours circulated about him were that he had a Chinese wife who spoke no English, that he lived with a transvestite and himself went in for cross-dressing, and that at home he scrubbed floors and acted as servant to a demanding mistress. I had no expectation of ever being able to verify such stories, and was surprised when during a lunch time session at the Plough he asked if I would be free to have dinner one evening. Surprise turned to astonishment when he elaborated.

'At home, I mean. Just a simple meal. My mother would like to meet you.' Why should his mother want to meet me? His manner seemed to preclude questioning.

We went out to Hammersmith by bus. He lived in a small terrace house in one of the nondescript streets off Dawes Road. (They have been tarted up now.) In the entrance hall there was a curious aseptic smell. Norris called out 'Mother, we're home' in a voice unlike his own, the voice one might use to a child.

In such small houses, built originally for artisans, the front room was kept as a parlour used only for visitors, and it was this door he now opened to reveal what might almost have been a little Victorian parlour, with many photographs on the walls, various tiny trinket boxes and small jugs on and around the mantelpiece, and in a walnut easy chair with ornate cabriole legs a white-haired lady who said how pleased she was to see me – and smiled as she wagged a hook at me instead of a hand. A glance, which I found myself unable to avoid, showed a companion hook replacing her left hand, both arms ending at the elbows.

We are used now to thalidomide babies grown to adulthood who are wonderfully dexterous in using hooks or other substitutes for hands, but at the time those hooks had all my attention, so that I barely noticed the small pretty face much like her son's, the carefully coiffed white hair, the blouse frilled at neck and sleeves or the blouse's ornamental buttons.

She said to her son, 'Norrie, everything's put out, we're

ready for our little drinkie.' And to me, 'Norrie's such a good boy, he does look after his poor old mum.' Her voice was pure Cockney, overlaid with veneers of both gentility and modernity. Norris went out, and returned a minute or two later with a tray containing three glasses and bottles of fino and amontillado sherry. 'I like the sweet myself, but I know the gentlemen prefer the dry.' Or in Norris's case whisky or beer, I thought as she hooked a claw round her glass. 'Chin chin', she said before taking the first sip.

And for Norris it was only a sip, after which he disappeared. His mother said, 'I admire your book so very very much.'

So that was the answer – I was in the presence of a fan, something not unknown to me, although then they were numbered in single spies. But still, I was surprised by her use of the singular, for even that many years ago I had written several books. Her next remark made things no clearer. 'Of course he is not a Catholic, the naughty boy, so he can't appreciate it as he should. But I know he admires it, of course he does.'

A devout atheist all my adult life, I stared at her, at a loss to know what she was talking about. She saw my incomprehension but misinterpreted it, though her next words made her meaning painfully clear.

'You must be one yourself to have written about an errant soul with such understanding.' And in a silvery artificial voice she quoted almost verbatim the last lines of *The Quest For Corvo*, the biography by my brother AJ of the homosexual would-be priest Frederick Rolfe. AJ died in 1941, and over the years I have received a number of letters written under the impression that I was the author of *The Quest For Corvo*, but a person-to-person error of this kind was new to me. I explained, stumblingly no doubt, that I was not the right Symons, had done no more than write an introduction to my brother's biography. She listened, disbelievingly as it seemed to me, then took a handkerchief from a small bag on her lap, put it to her eyes and hurried out of the room. I was left alone with the Victoriana.

Five minutes later Norris came in, and asked what I had said to upset his mother. I explained, adding that he might have told me she was expecting to meet the author of *The Quest For Corvo*.

'I didn't know that. I mentioned your name, and mother said she admired you and wanted to meet you. She reads a great deal', he said, as if that excused her mistake. 'And she becomes very absorbed in anything she enjoys. She takes part in it, if you see what I mean.'

'But she is a Catholic?'

'Only for the time being. If she reads a book about Bonnie Prince Charlie next month she may become a Jacobite. She's gone up to her room now, she gets upset very easily. I don't know if she'll come down to dinner.'

He spoke as if this were my fault, and glared at me when I asked if she had suffered an accident. 'We don't talk about it', he said, and I learned nothing more.

It was a dreadful evening. Norris and I ate our first course, watery soup, on our own and in almost total silence. His mother came down for the shepherd's pie and apple crumble that followed. Nothing more was said about Catholicism or *The Quest For Corvo*, but she made sprightly conversation about the iniquity of Malcolm Muggeridge's recent attack on the Royal family, the confidence we should all feel in delightful Sir Anthony Eden as Prime Minister, the increasing cost of all sorts of household goods which was something mere men didn't realise, and so on. Norris stayed determinedly silent, head down into shepherd's pie, so that I was left to murmur assent with views I disagreed with, and express interest in things I cared nothing about. It may be said that I had a choice, could have expressed robust support for the Nye Bevan wing of the Labour Party, but after the distress caused by my mistaken identity it seemed wrong to risk any further upset. Afterwards Norris walked with me to my bus stop. He remained silent until we had reached it, then said 'She did say she wanted to meet you. I'm sorry it didn't work out.'

I said it didn't matter, and couldn't resist asking what she thought about the *New Outlook*. 'She doesn't mention it. She's seen copies of course, but I think she's managed to blot it out of her mind. In a day or two she'll have forgotten the mistake she made about you, probably forgotten you altogether. It's a great gift really.' I said it must make life difficult for him at times. 'Oh, I don't know. My father died when I was ten, and I've always looked after her. She's like a child in many ways, we never argue, what would be the point, it would only upset her.'

At that point my bus arrived. Norris never referred to the visit afterwards. It lingered in my memory, however, the contrast between the stern though never authoritarian figure who occupied the oddly-shaped office at the paper and was regarded with awe even by the barmaids at the Plough, and the submissive son who must have sacrificed his emotional life to the care of his mother. I felt it was the basis for a crime story, although it was one I never wrote. Perhaps the personal life in Norris was sublimated successfully, perhaps for all of us such personal matters are less important in shaping our lives than we think them to be. Certainly it was social and not personal changes that shaped the fate of Norris Tibbs.

During the long years of Tory government in the Fifties and early Sixties, Leftish and politically liberal magazines lost both circulation and emotional impetus. In those years the process began in which reporters for daily and Sunday papers, with no particular beliefs but keen noses for scandal, exposed the political fiddling and behind the scenes Government manipulation that in earlier days Left-wing weeklies had regarded as their exclusive province. In addition they drew aside the curtain hiding dubious trade union practices which the weeklies had been much less ready to lift. In due course the investigatory zest spread to TV and radio, and nowadays the politico-arts journals have little reason for existence, replaced at one end of the spectrum by papers that invite libel actions like *Private Eye*, at the other by magazines of a specialised or academic kind. In the Fifties few foresaw such an outcome. It was a decade when the *New Statesman* was strongly on course for a hundred thousand circulation, though even there it was felt the time had come for Kingsley Martin to be replaced by John Freeman, who was linked not only with politics but with the comparatively new medium of television.

The magical six figures was reached under Freeman, but not for long. Within a few years the *New Statesman* was affected by the cold winds of the new journalism, to the extent of appointing Bruce Page, one of the most thrusting new journalists, as editor. The *New Outlook* felt the wind sooner and more keenly. It had been more closely connected with Labour in power, and once they were out of office the editorials and political articles that had been so closely scanned seemed not much more than the vapourings of the dispossessed saying how they would have managed things if the electorate had been wiser. At every weekly meeting, Norris said, it was agreed that the paper needed shaking up, a phrase that induced a burst of his rare laughter. 'You can shake up a kaleidoscope and the pieces drop into a different pattern, but they're still the same pieces', he said. Uttered in the Plough, to an admiring and mostly youthful audience, this seemed a profound truth, and certainly the replacement of amiable Joss Bedford by the strongly Bevanite MP, C. K. Chambers, seemed at first to make little difference.

Chambers looked like a bookkeeper or a junior accountant. He was pale, spectacled, and wore dark grey or dark blue suits rather than the jackets and pullovers favoured by VR and Joss Bedford. His appearance to some extent belied his character, which was that of a Robespierrean heresy hunter rather than a junior accountant. He had spent a month or two in Spain during the Civil War as an observer for one of the many groups gathering arms and financial support for the Republic, and was said to have returned with reports on the unreliable nature of some comrades. Was Chris (his unsuitable name) a closet Communist? There was no proof of this, although like his nearest Parliamentary associates D.

N. Pritt and Konni Zilliacus he was very much in favour of the Soviet Union on any issue where it clashed with the West.

I met him at a small office party to celebrate his arrival. He smiled grimly, said he understood I had once been a Trotskyite and hoped I wouldn't voice any opinions of that sort in the paper. At his first meeting with Norris he said he had great respect for the arts section, but it should be more directly linked to the paper's political line. Norris replied that he was responsible for what appeared.

'Of course. But I should like you to bear in mind that our purpose is the return of a Labour government. That's the paper's reason for being. Reviews like the one last week about Matthew Arnold are hardly likely to help.'

Such an observation must have been exquisitely painful for Norris, since he agreed with the thinking behind it. Like tight-lipped Chris he wanted more than anything to see the wicked cast out and the virtuous resume their proper places in the seats of power, and realised also that the cost of this must be acceptance of literature as a product of social use rather than something that might lift the spirit in a way independent of such a consideration. Indeed, I daresay that in theory he'd have gone along with the quite usual pragmatic (or Stalinist) idea of the time that nothing in life or in art could be considered independent of the concept of social use. When it came down to cases, though, Norris was absolutely unprepared to see a biography of Matthew Arnold ignored in favour of a book about Growth and Expansion in the Nationalised Industries, or to give a new collection of Auden's poems less space than a history of the National Union of Miners. He simmered with discontent, and was not pleased when I reminded him of past remarks about Socialist Philistines. He looked deep into his beer, and said there were worse things than Philistines. What could be worse? Norris consulted his beer again. 'Tories. Better the worst Socialist Philistine than the Tory who knows Shakespeare's sonnets by heart.'

He had his usual audience when the remark was made, and somebody said 'Like Samuel Butler.' Norris brushed aside the name as irrelevant. I wondered what Norris's mother would have said if she had heard her son. One of the young admirers asked what was so wrong with intelligent Tories. If they were intelligent, perhaps they might be converted? Norris shook his head.

'You know those lines of Auden's? "The earth obeys the intelligent and evil till they die"? They are intelligent but evil, sometimes do the right things but always for the wrong ends.'

In those days such quotations from Auden were taken almost as ultimate truths, and the young admirer was silenced. I suggested that Norris would prefer reactionary Dostoevsky to progressive Sholokhov. He looked at me gloomily, and said of course Dostoevsky was a great writer.

Norris's bickering with Chambers became more than that with the two invasions, that of the British at Suez and the Russians in Hungary. The first interested Norris very little, although he said it was a botched job, but the second appalled him. The pictures of tanks in the streets of Budapest, the death of Pal Maleter, the final despairing broadcast of Imre Nagy and his eventual execution, turned Norris's habitual gloomy calm into despair. George Constant, Georgie boy, had left the paper some while back but kept in touch with it, and it was he who told me of Norris's distress, and said he thought of resigning.

'It would be awful if he did, Norris has this terrific integrity. I'm not a thinker, you know that, but I've always looked up to Norris. Did you know the Beaver wanted him? Asked me to sound Norris out and I did, but he said no, just like that, didn't even want to know what was on offer. Not like me, tempted and fell.' Georgie's laugh showed his splendid teeth. 'I'm worried about him. Why don't you go round and see him, he likes you.'

I found Norris in the Plough, drinking whisky instead of beer, a bad sign. The term red-eyed is a cliche, but the rims of his eyes really were red. He bought me a drink. 'Have you seen the filthy *Morning Star*? What I say is fuck Dutt. Fuck

Dutt, fuck Dutt, fuck Dutt.' He had a deep aversion to Palme Dutt, the leading Party theoretician, and attributed to him the Party line on Hungary, which of course was that the Soviet tanks had gone in to stop emergent Fascist groups from taking power. I asked what he thought about the *New Outlook*'s editorials, which had wavered from cautious approval of the Nagy reforms to acceptance of the need for the Soviet invasion, plus a pious hope that the 'Russian presence in the country' would be removed once 'Socialist democracy had been restored'.

'Shit. Invertebrates. No backbone.' He paused. 'Fuck Chambers, fuck them all, what do they care about Socialism. I'm resigning.' I said I had heard a rumour he might go to a Beaverbrook paper as literary editor.

He shook his head. 'I'm a Socialist. What room is there for a Socialist on a Beaverbrook paper?' I mentioned Michael Foot, Tom Driberg, Georgie boy. 'Not like me. No room for somebody like me.' I recognised the truth of this. It was hard to imagine him lasting more than a few weeks on the *Daily* or *Sunday Express*.

'And mother's ill. You've met her. That was a mistake, sorry.' I asked what was wrong. 'Something inside, we don't talk about it. I've always looked after her, you know, can't think what I shall do without her.' I would have thought it a blessing to be relieved of his mother's conversation, but said only that I was sorry. He nodded. I never saw Norris drunk, but realised when he said I should come back to the office with him and have it out with Chris Chambers, that he was not exactly sober. I demurred, he was insistent, and in the end I went round with him under the impression that I might be of use as an intermediary. Norris did not tell me why he wanted me there, any more than he had said why his mother had wished to meet me.

We went up in the antiquated lift, and he made straight for the editor's office. Chambers's secretary, a girl named Sally Perkins whose pop eyes gave her the look of a startled faun, said Chris was busy. Norris jerked a thumb. 'Somebody in there?'

'No, but he's writing an editorial.'

Norris muttered something inaudible, advanced past her, flung open the door and announced 'Here he is.' Chris Chambers looked up, frowning. His desk was as neat as his person, a square writing pad on the blotter in front of him. An absurdly small clay pipe was stuck in the corner of his mouth.

'Say it to him.' Norris did the thumb jerking again, and I realised that 'Here he is', which I had thought referred to Chris on the lines of 'Ah, here you are', applied in fact to me. Norris now advanced to the desk and gave it a thump with his small fist, so that a brass letter opener with 'Blackpool' written on it bounced up and down. 'Say it to his face.'

Chambers removed the clay pipe, placed it carefully in the ashtray. His thin mouth almost vanished, thin eyebrows were raised. He gestured at the papers in front of him. 'I'm very busy.'

Norris turned to me. 'He says your review's got to come out, can't be used, against policy.'

I understood then why Norris had wanted me with him. Christopher Hollis had just published a book about Orwell and I had reviewed it in terms unfavourable to the book – Hollis seemed to regard Orwell as a Christian gone astray – but full of praise for Orwell, in particular for his uncompromising opposition to Stalinism, in the Soviet Union and nearer home. I could see that at this moment the review might be an embarrassment, and sure enough Chambers confirmed the thought.

'With all due respect, Norris, that is not what I said. I suggested this was not the right time to print such a review—'

'Give it back to him, you said, ask him to rewrite it.'

'Not at all. I suggested Julian might like to look at it again. As it stands the review might seem more at home in a paper of different complexion, the *Telegraph* perhaps.'

Norris's voice was raised to a shout. 'You're questioning the integrity of my reviewers, that means you're questioning mine too.'

'With due respect, that's nonsense.'

'To say I'd commission a review suitable for the *Telegraph*—'

'Norris, I told you I was busy. If you've got a complaint bring it up at next week's meeting. In the meantime the review will not go in. Do I make myself clear?'

Norris left muttering about dictatorship, and saying if the review was censored he would resign. I felt I had played the role of a dummy in the scene, and was not pleased with Norris for having kept me in the dark about what had happened, though Chambers's reluctance to print the piece made me angry. I put Norris's belligerence down to drink, and was surprised when he rang me a few days later to say his complaint to the quartet of MPs and academics who made up the paper's board had been rejected, and he had resigned. After telling me this he added, 'By the way, my mother died last Sunday', and put down the receiver before I could say anything. I was left with the uneasy feeling of guilt that is often felt after failure to perform some unspecifiable action that might have been ineffectual but would have served as a purge for conscience. The review appeared a month later, uncut.

I often thought about Norris in the following weeks, wondered if he was still living in the little house off Dawes Road, and what job he was doing. Nobody telephoned from the paper to offer me books for review and, always alert to the whiff of ostracism, I assumed that Chambers had placed an interdict on me after the Orwell piece. In the end I went round to Chancery Lane, up in the lift, turned right for literature, and – there was Norris. He greeted me with unusual warmth. I said I thought he had resigned.

'So I did. But they decided they couldn't do without me.' He managed to say this without a smile – he was not much of a smiler – yet without a trace of self-satisfaction. 'When *he* went they asked me to come back. Glad to see you. Thought you might not want to write for us again after the way you were treated.'

I said I'd had reviews spiked in the past, let alone had them appear late. I said I was a professional, and Norris nodded. Professionalism in this sense was alien to him, the idea that the spiking of reviews might be accepted as part of journalistic life not something he cared to contemplate. I asked what had happened to Chris Chambers.

'Gone. Let's have a jar round the corner, I'll tell you about it.'

In the darkness of the Plough he told me. Chambers had been brought in to check the slide in circulation, but under his editorship it had accelerated, and the board had been alarmed by a graph made by a mathematically-inclined sociologist showing the steepening rate of decline. Evidently the paper's readers didn't want articles about housing developments in the West Midlands or discussions of Socialism in Third World countries. Chambers was discarded, the quartet decided to run the papers themselves for the time being, and invited Norris to return.

I congratulated him, and was about to express sympathy regarding his mother when he said, 'I got married last week. To Brenda Dodd, we'd known each other some time. She does research for the TUC. You'll meet her, we're having a bit of a party.' More congratulations. I asked if he had moved. 'No need. Perfectly good house.'

The party was held in an upper room of a Fleet Street pub. Brenda was a tall horse-faced woman with a black patch over one eye, which I learned had been accidentally shot by a brother when she was a child. Was Norris attracted to women physically impaired? Perhaps. From the way in which Brenda ordered him about it was plain that she would run his home life for him as his mother had done in the past. Perhaps that also was what he wanted.

The following two years were probably the happiest of Norris's life. He was given extra space for special numbers and for theatre and film reviews (I was for a short time the paper's film reviewer), and allowed to run the book pages as he pleased. The front part of the paper was erratically edited, according to which members of the quartet had the upper hand. Brenda produced articles and reviews, the articles always including tables and sometimes graphs, the reviews written in the clogged dense language of the trade union bureaucrat, to which in her case Norris seemed oblivious. At the end of the two years, however, the board became aware that the circulation decline had been slowed but not halted. It was time for another shake up, time for experiment, for a new editor who would be in touch with a new decade. Or so the quartet thought.

The man they chose was Thurston Lacey.

'Have you heard of him?' Norris asked. 'Neither had I. They say he's a live wire. The way he looked at me I could see he thought I was dead wood. He says he won't interfere, but he's got *ideas*.' What sort of ideas? 'In the front end there's to be a regular page called "The Feminine Angle" with a different woman writing it each week, and a sort of gossip column called "Newscount".' And the back pages? Norris changed his voice to a ridiculous mock-Bloomsbury treble. 'I'll be frank and say I feel they're just, well, old-fashioned. I'd like to include pictures to break up those masses of type that look, let's be frank, *solid*. Then I think we ought to go for what's new, what's buzzing, with not too much discussion of Eng Lit and dear old crusty Leavis. How's about Salinger, Bellow, James Baldwin, how's about comparing them with the young English angries? How's about a column called "These Authors Make To-Morrow's News"? He really said that, Julian.'

'About making to-morrow's news?'

'No no. He really said "How's about", said it twice. I said I should run the pages the way I wanted and he said, of course, he was just thinking off the top of his head. I wish the top of his head would blow off. I fear the worst.'

I said the worst never happened, but it did. I was doing research for a book about the South African war, spending days among War Office papers and in the London Library, so that I saw nothing of Norris. It was Georgie boy, on the way up the ladder to his knighthood but still keeping a toehold on the past, who told me what happened.

'Thurston is with it, you know, he's been around Fleet Street, drama critic of the *Mail*, wrote the Hickey column for a while. He knows what sells, he's *there*, he's to-morrow's man.' I asked if he was a Socialist. 'Not Norris's sort, but he votes Labour like me. Thurston says he won't interfere with the back end of the paper, but of course he does, first a column about "What's On In The Arts", then getting a couple of big name reviewers Norris couldn't say no to since the paper pays peanuts – but you know that. The crux came when Thurston put up to Norris the idea of a series called something like "The Arts To-day and To-morrow", with people like Reyner Banham on architecture, some American named Greenberg saying hurrah for abstract art, and so on. Norris turned it down flat, as Thurston knew he would, Thurston took it to the quartet, they said wonderful, goodbye Norris. Simple operation. Sad, but it had to happen. Let's face it, Norris belongs to the past, I couldn't use him on any of my papers.'

The story of the *New Outlook*'s rise in circulation under Thurston Lacey, its later hiccup and eventual amalgamation with the monthly *New Worlds* doesn't belong here, since this piece is about Norris. A few months after he had left the paper a few of us who had known him well gave him dinner at Bertorelli's, including Elsie Smith, Osbert Winkle, Georgie boy, and of course black-patched Brenda. The freedom of the Sixties was gathering strength and momentum, with *That Was The Week* on TV, and verbal freedom already greatly enlarged by the result of the *Lady Chatterley* trial. I had reported on the case for the *Sunday Times*, along with Ken Tynan and Bernard Levin, writing for the *Observer* and *Spectator*. All three of us, as we looked at the jury, felt they would condemn the book, though from my recollection only Tynan and I said so in print. In our articles all three of us said hurrah for a famous victory, hurrah for the freedom of art.

Norris ate little but drank a lot that evening, first whisky and then wine, ignoring an occasional dissuasive word from Brenda. When somebody mentioned the case he turned on me, and said I should be ashamed of the stuff I'd written. Osbert asked if he was in favour of censorship, and Norris became eloquent.

'Is *Lady Chatterley* a great novel? Of course not, none of you will pretend it is. Is it important it should be published just because there are words in it not usually printed? Again of course not. You want it printed in the name of freedom, but you're Socialists like me, and I tell you such freedom has nothing to do with Socialism.'

He glared round the table. Elsie asked, spacing out the words carefully, if he was saying freedom had nothing to do with Socialism.

'Not this silly freedom. Not the freedom to say knickers and make sniggering jokes about religion on that deadly box, not freedom to copulate with fifty people in a week. If that's freedom, why don't we all get into one great bed and fuck one another?' One or two people at other tables looked round in amusement. Brenda said *hush*. Norris lowered his voice. 'Socialism means order, reason, good sense, a fair division of the cake. Liberty, equality, fraternity, yes, but the greatest of these is equality. Liberty, the disgusting liberty that man has brought to my paper, the schoolboy liberty to read dirty words, comes a long way behind.'

'Shall I tell you what I see in the future?' Nobody liked to stop him. 'I see your freedom spreading like a disease. Freedom to print anything anywhere, to scribble obscenities in churches and classrooms, choose what you want to learn instead of being taught, copulate indiscriminately, old and young, men with men and women with women. That man is homosexual.' (We understood he could not bring himself to name Thurston.) 'I see all kinds of nonsense called art, any daub or cartoon or children's comic book. Any half-baked piece of verbal trickery will be called an experimental novel. All this will be done and said in the sacred name of freedom,

137

some of it in the name of Socialism, but it will have nothing to do with Socialism and there is nothing sacred about freedom. All freedom must be limited, and the proper limits can only be set through Socialism. Anything else is rubbish.' He waved a hand, knocked over a glass. 'That man and his friends will encourage the rubbish, and people like you will take it seriously. Yeats had a line for it: "Mere anarchy is loosed upon the world."'

He had spoken with perfect clarity, but now lowered his head on the table and began to snore. Elsie said 'Poor Norris', Osbert Winkle 'Yesterday's Socialist is to-morrow's Fascist.' Brenda got to her feet, adjusted her eye patch, and asked if one of us would help her get Norris home.

Six months later he died from cirrhosis of the liver. Looking back on that evening I see the force of Osbert Winkle's comment, yet it seems to me that most of Norris's prophecies came true.